"Are You Sure I Can't Persuade You to Come with Me?"

he murmured, leaning closer.

Even as Marnie shook her head in denial, she found herself warming to the fire kindling in his dusky eyes. Without protest, she allowed herself to be gathered into his embrace. Eager lips explored hers, moving slowly over her mouth with tantalizing tenderness. She felt herself begin to respond to him with a surge of yearning that startled her with its intensity. As if it was the most natural thing in the world, she arched her body against his and wrapped her arms around his waist, drawing him against her.

He raised his head to gaze down at her, triumph shining in his dark eyes. "Now tell me that you won't come with me," he muttered thickly. "Tell me you don't have time to share my bed!"

TIFFANY PAYNE

loves romances so much that she started out her career working as a sales representative, traveling to various bookstores with Silhouette Books. She has recently settled down to write in her home along the picturesque coast of Mississippi.

Dear Reader:

I'd like to take this opportunity to thank you for all your support and encouragement of Silhouette Romances.

Many of you write in regularly, telling us what you like best about Silhouette, which authors are your favorites. This is a tremendous help to us as we strive to publish the best contemporary romances possible.

All the romances from Silhouette Books are for you, so enjoy this book and the many stories to come.

Karen Solem
Editor-in-Chief
Silhouette Books

TIFFANY PAYNE
Stirrings of the Heart

Silhouette Romance

Published by Silhouette Books New York

America's Publisher of Contemporary Romance

SILHOUETTE BOOKS, a Division of Simon & Schuster, Inc.
1230 Avenue of the Americas, New York, N.Y. 10020

Copyright © 1984 by Tiffany Payne

Distributed by Pocket Books

ISBN: 0-671-57283-0

First Silhouette Books printing March, 1984

10 9 8 7 6 5 4 3 2 1

Map by Ray Lundgren

America's Publisher of Contemporary Romance

Printed in the U.S.A.

BC91

Stirrings of
the Heart

Chapter One

The narrow path lazily meandered through acres of green meadows dotted with silver-leafed olive trees. Behind her fashionable sunglasses, Marnie Chandler's emerald eyes shone with pleasure at the enchanting beauty of Crete. The sultry Mediterranean sun bathed her lightly clad body with warmth and sent her spirits soaring as she made her way down the rugged hillside.

The morning stillness echoed with the soft patter of her Italian sandals. The only other sound was the occasional muted tinkle of a sheep's bell in the distance. Circled by a thin gold bracelet, her slender wrist swung in unison with her confident strides. Marnie slowed to a stop as the worn path under her feet suddenly forked off in divergent directions.

The faint yet distinctive stirrings of the sea were unmistakable in the distance. She couldn't be far from the cove now, she told herself as she checked her bearings. The broad, blue expanse of the Mediterranean twinkled through the gaps of the grove of olive trees to her left. A smile of anticipation curved her lips as she headed down the path leading to the shore.

This secluded cove promised all of the relaxing tranquillity that she could desire. Heaven knows she deserved it after the frantic pace of the last month. Proctoring final exams, grading term papers and preparing for a trip abroad had kept her constantly on the go. It was a schedule calculated to make even the most devoted archaeology professor yearn for summer recess.

Marnie's first year as an instructor at the university had been every bit as fulfilling and successful as she could have wished. It had been quite a feather in her cap when the prestigious Cincinnati school had offered such a coveted entry-level position to the young Ph.D. from Chicago. She had headed for southern Ohio without a backward glance, vowing to make the most of this splendid chance to establish herself at the distinguished university. Her hard work had been rewarded by her recent promotion to assistant professor. Now, at twenty-four, she was the youngest tenured professor in her department.

She had earned this vacation and was eager to spend her first day exploring the sun-dappled island of Crete. A bracing swim in the waters of the fabled Mediterranean would be the perfect introduction to Greece, and not a bad way to begin a working vacation, she admitted with a cheerful smile.

The aquamarine water sparkled as she reached the strip of white-sand beach. The crystal-blue waves swirled at her feet, beckoning in seductive rhythm with their undulating rush to the shore. Kicking off her sandals, Marnie slipped out of her apricot-colored beach jacket. Her matching bikini revealed a slender yet shapely figure still pale from the chill of a Midwestern winter.

Turning her delicately sculptured features to face the open sea, she closed her eyes and filled her lungs with the pungent salt air. She stood motionless, savoring the coarseness of the sun-bleached sand beneath her bare toes.

"You've waited years for this, Marnie," she whispered. She had dreamed of such a pilgrimage to Greece ever since the days of her first undergraduate archaeology course. The study of ancient cultures and people had sparked her interest then, developing in swift order into the commitment necessary to sustain her throughout the rigors of graduate school. Those early college days seemed light years away now.

Perching her hands on her hips, she surveyed the crescent-shaped length of the cove with obvious delight. As her shining eyes scanned the shoreline, an urgent flicker of movement down the beach seized her attention. Catching her breath with a small gasp, she stared in amazement.

A large, gray rock, similar to dozens scattered haphazardly around the sand, was thrashing wildly near the water's edge. Puzzled, Marnie frowned in disbelief. The rock seemed to be alive! Prodded by intense curiosity, she started down the beach for a closer look. All movement ceased as she halted a few yards away.

Her eyes darkened with concern as she suddenly realized that the gray mound was an enormous fish—a dolphin. She recognized the sleek, streamlined shape of the mammal from childhood trips to an aquarium with her parents.

Edging closer, she regarded the motionless creature lying at her feet with heartfelt sympathy. She had read stories about whales that unwittingly beached themselves on the sand when their natural sonar systems went haywire. Unless they were returned to the water in a very short period of time, they were doomed to die on dry land. Marnie didn't need to be told that this dolphin was in serious danger. Its labored breathing underscored its critical condition.

She knelt down on one knee to touch the sleek gray flesh. The skin felt hot and dry under her fingertips. Impulsively wading into the surf, she cupped her hands together and began splashing a cascade of water over its parched body.

When both she and the dolphin were dripping wet, she paused, pursing her lips in thought. That would only suffice as a stopgap measure. Eyeing the creature's form, she estimated that it must be almost five feet from the tip of the protruding snout to the graceful tail. Its dead weight would require brute strength to budge it even an inch. She didn't have a hope of moving the creature by herself.

She brushed a stray wisp of hair from her cheek as she glanced around the cove, praying for some form of help. From the corner of her eye, she caught a swift flutter of motion up on the ridge of the hill. Spinning around in that direction, she stared in disappointment at the empty hilltop. Whatever it was, it had vanished. It might have been her imagination, but she would have sworn that she had seen the figure of a man. Had someone been standing there silently watching her? With a gesture of impatience, she turned back to the dolphin.

There was only one thing that she could do. She would have to follow the path back up the hill and summon help from the hotel. It would take time, but she had no other choice. She couldn't just stand by and allow such a magnificent creature to perish in front of her eyes. A sob rose in her throat. It was up to her to save this dolphin!

"Hold on, fella," she encouraged the listless dolphin. "I'll be back as fast as I can."

The intensifying heat of the clear June morning hampered her pace, but with a pounding heart she pushed on to the top of the hill. Panting, she stopped at the crest to gulp several lungfuls of the tangy sea air. From where she stood the dolphin's form was indistinguishable from the clusters of gray rock scattered along the shoreline far below.

As Marnie turned to race on her way, the sound of a low whinny stopped her. Squinting against the sun's glare, she glanced around her.

A few yards away, she spied a handsome palomino stallion saddled and tethered to the outstretched limb of an olive tree. Munching a mouthful of tender leaves, the animal studied her from the depths of huge, cocoa-brown eyes.

Marnie searched the area around the stallion hoping to spot its rider, but the silent path stretched empty before her. The thyme-scented meadow echoed only with the drone of honey bees and the whisper of the wind. She remembered that it was common in Greece to let animals graze by themselves at the side of a trail. She had seen donkeys and sheep alone by the roadside on her drive from the airport in Iráklion to the hotel yesterday.

As she frowned at the palomino, she suddenly realized that such a strapping animal would surely be strong enough to drag the dolphin off the beach. No one would be the wiser if she borrowed the horse for a few minutes. She would save precious time this way. It might be her only chance to save the dolphin. . . .

"Easy, boy. Steady now," she coaxed. Reassured by the stallion's placid acceptance of her hand on the reins, Marnie turned to examine a coil of rope sticking out of the chamois saddlebag. There was plenty of rope, she told herself with a satisfied smile. This was going to be as easy as pie.

As she led the horse down the path, she idly admired the elegant scrollwork carved into the expensive leather of the saddle. Running her eyes over the palomino's polished golden coat, she knew its rider must take great pride in its striking appearance.

"What would your owner think if he knew that you were going to be a hero?" she teased the prancing animal. "I wager he'd be proud of you."

But a few seconds later, her lighthearted vivacity was dashed when a piercing whistle sliced through the air behind them. Pricking its delicate ears, the stallion halted in its tracks. The animal's unexpected balk caught Marnie off balance, pushing her forcefully to the ground.

"Now what!" she exclaimed, dusting off her smarting knees. Picking up her crumpled jacket from beneath the horse's hooves, she wrapped the loose folds over her shoulders. From her kneeling position, she glanced around the woods, catching her breath with a gasp as her eyes focused on the tall, muscular man pursuing them down the slope.

His trim, powerful body moved with an athlete's easy grace and style. A white knit shirt molded smoothly over the rigid contours of his towering six-foot frame. The buttons at his throat were left carelessly open, revealing a thick mat of ebony hair against the solid expanse of his bronzed chest. A rawhide belt spanned his tapered waist, and snug-fitting jeans hugged his narrow hips and corded thighs. He wore a Greek fisherman's cap perched on his dark head in a jaunty fashion, casting an ominous shadow over his chiseled features.

Suppressing a shiver of apprehension, Marnie bit her lip. A belated twinge of conscience made her realize that she had not for a second considered that she might get caught with the borrowed stallion. Her motives were entirely aboveboard, but now she would have to waste valuable time explaining herself to this stranger.

Judging from his clenched fists and steely expression, she acknowledged that it might take some effort to calm such a commanding giant. He looked like the type who would shoot first and ask questions later, she thought, narrowing her eyes in cool assessment. There was no choice but to meet him head-on.

She rose to her feet and squared her shoulders as he halted only inches from her. For a long moment, they stared at each other wordlessly. The lilting song of a wild thrush trickled into the stony silence between them.

"Where in the blazes do you think you're going with my horse?" he challenged in English. His mellow baritone was laced with prickly irritation.

Without waiting for an answer, his eyes abruptly shifted to check the stallion. Marnie welcomed the opportunity to examine his granitelike features at close range. She noted the annoyance radiating from his intelligent, deep-set eyes, their smoky depths flecked with volcanic sparks of auburn. His forceful chin gave him an unyielding almost ruthless air, though the impression was tempered slightly by the generous curve of his arrogant lips. His coal-black hair glistened with the lustrous highlights of robust health and was accented by a narrow fringe of premature silver at his temples.

It was the face of a man who confronted life boldly, with no excuses for his actions, a man who wouldn't beat around the bush but would live his life according to his own terms. With a tiny frown, she realized that he looked vaguely familiar.

"Cat got your tongue, little thief?" he taunted. His restless gaze flickered over her face, examining the flawless complexion, delicate bones and pert tilt of her nose. Although her features lacked the perfect symmetry of classic beauty, the warmth and spirit glowing from Marnie's emerald eyes had captured the admiration of more than one man.

"I need to borrow your horse," Marnie responded to

his jibe with icy forcefulness. "I would have asked permission, but there was no one around."

"Borrow!" he snarled in disbelief. "Horse thieves are not tolerated in these parts, young woman. I've caught you red-handed!" His eyes roamed over the generous curves of her body. "I ought to teach you a lesson you'll never forget."

She stiffened at his barbed threat. Releasing her hold on the stallion's reins, she planted both hands on her hips and glared at him with piercing directness. Their eyes locked in mutual contempt.

Marnie was suddenly aware of the fact that she wore only a wet, clinging bathing suit, marginally concealed by the loose folds of her jacket. Somehow, the stranger's brazen scrutiny made her feel naked and vulnerable.

Just who did he think he was? She simmered with red-hot anger. She could have conducted a more civilized conversation with the palomino.

For a split second her memory cleared, and she realized why his face had seemed so familiar. The last newspaper photos she remembered seeing of Ross Landry were several years old. They had portrayed a younger, more carefree man. He must be about thirty-five now, she estimated, but there was no mistaking those arrogant features. This was without a doubt the same maverick philanthropist who only a few years ago had been an anathema to scholars all over the world.

She remembered only too well the scandal that had erupted around the Landry-sponsored research team that claimed to have discovered the "lost" continent of Atlantis. For days they had basked in the international limelight provided by flotillas of reporters and photographers. Their much-heralded find was widely declared to be the most significant archaeological achievement in centuries.

But a short time later, things began to sour. While the celebrated "Atlantis" artifacts were being examined by experts and tested for authenticity, a museum curator had identified some of the articles as the same ones that had been stolen from an Athens museum only a few weeks earlier. Academics concerned with the integrity of professional research had joined forces to denounce the fraud, and an investigation had been launched by the Greek police. It had been months before the furor had died down.

Given his shady reputation, Marnie thought critically, she really shouldn't be surprised by Ross Landry's bullish behavior. He wasn't the sort of man she would willingly associate with, and he had some nerve accusing her of being a thief! What was he doing here, anyway? She wouldn't have thought that this quiet village in Crete would hold any attraction for a man like him.

With an impatient shake of her tawny mane, she brought her spiraling thoughts under control. She could worry about Ross Landry later. Right now the dolphin's plight was desperate, and she needed assistance —anyone's assistance.

"Look, there's a beached dolphin down in that cove. I was planning to use your horse to pull it off the sand. Can't we forgo the theatrics under the circumstances? Every second counts." Her assertive tone seemed to surprise him for an instant.

He responded with a slow grin. "So that's what you were doing down there on the beach. It looked as though you were splashing water on a rock. I thought you were just another dizzy tourist."

"So you were watching me! Well, I'm sorry to disappoint you," she pointed out acidly, "but I'm quite sane, just a normal, average woman."

"I certainly wouldn't describe you as average," he

replied, dazzling her with a smile. His wandering gaze lingered with frank appreciation on the rounded ripeness of her full breasts and then moved lower to take in her trim waist and shapely hips. "Not average at all," he repeated. "Are you here on vacation? Alone?" His hawklike scrutiny focused on the bare fingers of her left hand.

"You'd be a whiz guessing weights at a circus sideshow," she snapped. "If you're finished dissecting me now, do you think you could find it in your heart to help me with the dolphin?" It was impossible to hide the irritation in her tone. While he stood there leering at her, the dolphin's skin was broiling under the hot sun. Time was running out.

"My heart and body are yours for the asking, beautiful lady," he responded with mock gallantry. "But I'll reserve my soul until we're better acquainted."

"I'm not interested in your heart and soul, just your muscles," she countered. "Let's go!" There was no time to argue with his presumptuousness now. She would put him in his place later after the dolphin was rescued.

"Wait a minute." He grabbed her arm with gentle yet iron-like firmness. "We're going to put this on a first-name basis. I'm Ross Landry." He paused significantly.

"Marnie Chandler."

"Well, Marnie, I'll make you a deal." His smoky gaze sought hers. "I'll help you now if you'll have dinner with me tonight. We can discuss our plans for the summer with wine and candlelight," he hinted in a seductive tone.

"I wouldn't have dinner with you on a bet," she lashed out at him, anger cracking through her deliberate poise. "Your arrogance is astounding!"

"Come, come." He chuckled. "There's no such thing

as a free lunch, you know. If you want my help, you'll have to agree to my terms." He smiled down at her as if he were suggesting the most reasonable thing in the world.

"That's blackmail," Marnie accused tersely.

"Your vocabulary is a little harsh. Let's just say that if you rub my back, I'll rub yours."

"And if I don't?" Her green eyes darkened with the challenge. She didn't like the undercurrents of this conversation. In fact, she disliked Ross Landry intensely.

"The dolphin's fate rests in your hands," he said with a shrug. His hands perched against his lean hips with deceptive casualness. She could sense the leashed power in his muscular frame. It was almost like being stalked by a panther, she thought to herself. There was no doubt in her mind that he would make good on his threat if she refused the bargain.

There had to be a way to save the dolphin and teach him a lesson at the same time, she reasoned, slanting him a murderous glance. Ross obviously had no inkling of her professional connections. He hadn't even stipulated that they dine alone; he had simply assumed that she would be unaccompanied. Her innate common sense told her to let him have his hollow victory now. Tonight, when he tried to collect on the deal, would be soon enough for her revenge.

"Okay, you've talked me into it." She forced her lips to curve into a stiff smile. Under normal circumstances, she would feel distaste for such pretense, but these were not normal circumstances. She was going to enjoy leading the arrogant Ross Landry down the garden path. "I'll have dinner with you tonight, if you wish. But I do mean only dinner," she amended in a testy admonition.

"Well, that's a start," he declared with unshakable

good humor. "I'll just have to rely on my scintillating conversation and boyish charm to do the rest." His dark eyes danced with gentle self-mockery.

"You might just get more than you bargained for." Marnie nodded in bland agreement. Two could play this game as well as one, she realized with a burst of satisfaction.

"Let's go rescue that dolphin," he urged, adroitly taking charge of the situation. With an effortless motion, he mounted the frisky stallion and leaned down to offer her his hand. She wavered for only an instant before scrambling into the saddle behind him.

"Hold tight!" he warned, as the animal broke into a fast canter.

Hold tight, indeed. Marnie frowned. She wished that she could ignore the hard flesh beneath her fingers. Although she disliked admitting it, the intimate contact of their bodies was causing her pulse to race. Every nerve in her body was alert and tingling with excitement. It was purely a physical response, she reminded herself. Her poise was unthreatened. Ross Landry wasn't her type. After all, the man was a thief!

The worsening plight of the dolphin, however, immediately crowded out all other concerns. Within a matter of minutes, they had looped one end of the rope in a secure knot around the base of its tail. The opposite end was fastened to the horn of the palomino's saddle. United by a common feeling of urgency for the dolphin's well-being, they worked together in companionable silence.

Marnie found herself unexpectedly admiring the gentleness and patience that Ross displayed toward the frightened animal. With a velvet tone in his voice, he soothed and calmed the dolphin as they worked. It was a far cry from the outburst she had witnessed during the first minutes of their meeting. She wondered what other surprises might be lurking behind that hawklike expression.

To avoid hurting the dolphin, Ross led the stallion into the shallow water with deliberate care. As the rope stretched taut, the palomino strained to drag the helpless creature inch by inch off the sand. Marnie waded at its side, signaling to Ross when the water was deep enough for the dolphin to float. Her fingers fumbled with nervous excitement as she loosened the slip knot from around its tail. Together they turned the dolphin's head in the direction of the open sea.

It paused long enough to gulp a huge breath of air and then dived for the bottom. Its gray sleekness disappeared beneath the shimmering water before resurfacing several yards away. With the nimble grace of a dancer, the dolphin circled once around the spot where they stood, as if to say thanks. Then it headed for the freedom of the deep.

"Oh, how beautiful!" Marnie whispered breathlessly. She and Ross stood side by side watching for a last glimpse of the dolphin, but the blue waves washing against their legs seemed to have swallowed every trace.

"I've always believed that beauty is in the eye of the beholder." Ross's tone was as mellow and seductive as fine brandy. With a lazy, casual motion, he draped an arm over her bare shoulders, pulling her gently around to face him. "And I am privileged to behold you, pretty lady."

"I suppose you consider yourself a connoisseur," Marnie replied, arching her brows. Her mood was softened by the dolphin's successful rescue.

Holding her in the secure circle of his arms, he considered her words for a long moment. Her eyes were riveted to his strong features as she watched him trace the smooth contours of her face. His gaze lingered over her mouth, drinking in the allure of her moist red lips.

"As a man I know that you're not only beautiful, but passionate as well," he declared huskily.

"How can you be sure I'm not just another cold fish?" She couldn't resist mocking him.

"It's possible that no one has ever tempted you with the right bait," he parried. "But some fishermen are more skilled than others."

"I suppose that you're a master at casting lures," she challenged dryly. Male egos were all alike.

"I aim to do my best."

Marnie's growing curiosity about this enigmatic man held her motionless in his arms. She felt a tantalizing desire to sample his brand of passion for herself. After all, she reasoned, one kiss would not brand her for life. He simply wasn't her type. And giving in to him now could only make her revenge this evening that much sweeter.

His searching mouth found hers unerringly, caressing her soft lips until she relaxed against him with a languid sigh. The kiss grew in intensity as his lips coaxed hers with a tenderness that sent her blood soaring. As Marnie unconsciously arched her body against his, she heard him moan softly. He pulled her closer, pressing her against the rock-hardness of his thighs. His wandering hands moved lower, fondling the gentle curve of her waist.

"Let's go someplace where we'll be more comfortable," he murmured against her ear. His breath sent a dizzying warmth spiraling along her nerves, but his words were like a dash of ice water to her common sense. Fighting the vertigo threatening to engulf her, she pushed her palms firmly against the broad expanse of his chest.

"No!" she protested fiercely. "Our deal was for dinner, nothing else." Shaking her tawny locks out of her eyes, she glared up at him to reinforce her words. Her control had slipped, but only for a moment. The deliberate poise clicked back into place with smooth precision.

"Just let me whet your appetite now," he coaxed with husky persuasion. "I promise that the main course tonight will be unforgettable." His dark eyes watched her with the alertness of a hawk soaring above its prey.

"My appetite can wait until this evening." She shrugged her bare shoulders with a careless gesture. Although she couldn't deny his seductive power, she wasn't going to forget his unfair tactics in wrangling a dinner date. Or his dubious reputation. Despite her responsiveness to him, Ross Landry had some dues to pay. She returned his gaze without blinking.

"Then come, my little mermaid, let's return to dry land," he relented, sensing the strength of her determination. Circling her shoulders with a muscular arm, he steered her back toward the shore. The dripping palomino greeted them on the beach with an eager nicker.

Patting the proud arch of the animal's neck, Ross gathered up the reins and swung his lean frame into the saddle. Glancing down at Marnie, he tipped his hat in her direction with a jaunty sweep of his arm.

"You're staying at the hotel, I presume?" At her curt acknowledgment, he grinned devilishly. "Then I'll see you tonight at seven. Don't forget our bargain, Marnie Chandler."

"How could I ever forget such a deal?" She smiled up at him in mock sweetness. With a satisfied nod, he turned the palomino and headed back up the path.

"And don't think that I'm not going to relish every minute," she vowed softly to his back.

Chapter Two

The tingling spray splashed over Marnie's upturned face and down the slender length of her tanned body. Squeezing the tube of scented shower gel, she lathered and scrubbed away all lingering traces of sand and salt. The gentle buffing of the natural sea sponge in her hand made her flesh glow.

She had stayed at the cove far into the afternoon, indulging in the carefree pleasures of a beachcomber. The short nap she had snatched upon her return to the hotel had refreshed her normally high energy level. Now she felt ready to face anything, even her one-sided bargain with Ross Landry.

She could hardly wait to see the look on his arrogant face when she appeared for dinner in the company of Professor Richard Harte, her department chairman. As the president of a highly regarded society of archaeologists, the professor was sure to have neither forgotten nor forgiven the Atlantis scandal. No one connected with archaeology had been able to ignore the uproar it had created, and Marnie was thoroughly familiar with the professor's outspoken criticism of the flourishing black-market trade in stolen antiquities. In his opinion, the only people worse than the thieves themselves were the wealthy individuals who purchased such relics for their private collections. Ross's audacity in trying to pass the Atlantis articles off as legitimate finds could only be doubly offensive in the professor's eyes.

If everything proceeded as she hoped, the dinner conversation tonight would be distinctly uncomfortable for Ross. The evening would be a far cry from the seductive rendezvous of wine and candlelight he had proposed. Her lips curved into a smile as she savored the satisfaction it would give her to take some of the wind out of his sails.

Stepping out of the shower, she patted herself dry and pinned a small towel turban-style around her hair. She lightly dusted her skin with scented powder, then slipped into the silky folds of a brightly printed caftan.

She padded barefooted out of the bathroom and switched on a brass lamp at one end of the olive-wood dresser. Its cheery glow reflected twin pools of light on the white stucco ceiling and the dark parquet floor of the spacious room. Plush flokati rugs of woven sheep's hair lay scattered at her feet and near the brass bed and wicker loveseat. A huge bouquet of fresh wildflowers graced the antique pedestal table that was equipped with two comfortable chairs and a study lamp, perfect for a scholar's needs. The room's pastel hues of ivory and mint were a soothing contrast to the scorching fierceness of the Greek sun.

Marnie acknowledged that the hotel had been a pleasant surprise. She felt as though she were in residence at a luxurious Mediterranean villa rather than a village inn. She wondered how such an establishment had survived before the opening of the nearby dig. Even with the influx of researchers like herself and the professor, it must be difficult to make ends meet. Despite Ross's assumption that she was just another tourist, she suspected that sightseers were few and far between in this isolated area of Crete.

She dried her hair, then deftly braided the strands into a sophisticated twist. Securing the braid at the nape of her neck with delicate amber combs, she left only a few tendrils free to curl alluringly at her temples. She fastened the clasps of her favorite gold earrings and turned toward the walk-in closet.

There was no point in deliberately encouraging Ross's attentions by dressing up this evening, but she did like to look her best. Her wispy frock of lilac voile was perfect for the warm summer evening. The filmy fabric was subtly designed to attain just the right note of casual elegance. She would have worn this gown tonight anyway, she told herself with a shrug. Why change to something drabber just because of Ross's mocking gaze?

A pair of high-heeled Italian sandals complemented her chic yet very feminine appearance. A last glance in the mirror as she slipped out of the door assured her that the afternoon in the sun had warmed her cheeks with a flattering, natural blush.

The portly figure of Professor Harte was waiting as promised in the lobby near the foot of the marble stairway. Marnie had intentionally failed to mention Ross by name when she had spoken to the professor earlier in the afternoon. She was afraid that he might refuse her request if he knew of Ross's involvement. Instead, she had outlined the story of the dolphin and the conditions surrounding the dinner bargain. Teasingly reminding the professor that she was in Crete at his invitation, she had pleaded with him to lend his support to the evening. He had laughingly agreed.

"You look enchanting this evening, my dear. I think

the Mediterranean air agrees with you." The professor bent his snowy white head to give her a fatherly peck on the cheek.

"It's wonderful here, Professor. Sarah was correct. I'm going to hate leaving in only three weeks." She smiled up at his kindly face with genuine affection.

The professor and his wife Sarah had graciously opened their home to her when she had first arrived in Cincinnati. She and Sarah had since become close friends. Indeed, Marnie suspected that it had been Sarah who suggested the idea of her coming to Crete when the professor learned that his longtime associate, Roger Bass, would be delayed this season.

Marnie had jumped at the chance to collaborate on the professor's summer writing project for a prestigious academic journal. It meant her first trip to Greece—a mecca for archaeologists of all ages—as well as an opportunity for recognition in her field that any aspiring young professional would envy.

"This island is Sarah's favorite," the professor confided. "The stark beauty of the land and the simplicity of the people have always intrigued her. I guarantee that she wouldn't have missed this trip if it hadn't been for the birth of Ellen's baby, but she just couldn't bear to leave her new granddaughter at two weeks of age."

"I heard that you considered postponing the trip yourself until Sarah promised to take snapshots of the baby every single day," Marnie reminded him with a smile.

"Well, I did give her a new camera and a few extra rolls of film before I left," he admitted with a broad grin. "I naturally expect her to use them."

"Did you complete the outline you were working on this afternoon?" Marnie asked, her face revealing her eagerness to begin work on the project.

"No, I decided to follow the advice I had so wisely

given to you and postpone serious work until tomorrow. I confess I fell asleep next to the pool." His blue eyes crinkled with amusement as he regarded her over the top of his glasses. "I was simply exhausted from fielding questions about my lovely new associate. I must have promised at least a half dozen young researchers a personal introduction to you this evening."

"I'm sorry to spoil your matchmaking, Professor, but the lady is spoken for tonight." The velvety, baritone voice behind them resonated with male confidence.

Marnie felt a quiver of anticipation race down her spine as she glanced around to find Ross's brown eyes studying her. He stood only inches away, and she was struck once again by the sheer strength of his masculinity. He was clad in tailored beige slacks and an expensive continental-style navy blazer. The buttoned-down collar of his Oxford shirt added just a touch of Ivy League polish to his appearance. Ross Landry looked every inch the perfect gentleman she knew he was not!

Before Marnie could voice the appropriate flip response, however, she was stopped cold by the unexpected heartiness of the professor's greeting.

"My dear fellow, you are a sight for sore eyes! Your assistant swore that you were hard at work at a bankers' conference in Geneva. We didn't expect you for several days." He enthusiastically pumped Ross's outstretched arm.

"I finished my business early, Professor. And, believe me, Greek sun is far superior to Swiss rain. I came back this morning just in time to rescue a fair maiden in distress." Ross slanted a dark brow in Marnie's direction.

She returned his gaze with a defiant lift of her chin. "I had the situation well under control before you so rudely appeared," she reminded him curtly. "You could hardly label me a maiden in distress."

Despite her spunky words, she found it difficult to conceal a gnawing sense of disappointment. This wasn't the reception she had imagined between the two of them at all. She had expected sparks, if not fireworks. But instead, they had greeted each other like long-lost brothers. Glancing from Ross to the professor, Marnie realized that her plans for the evening were threatening to unravel right before her eyes.

"I'm sure that there are a host of students at the university who would agree with Marnie, Ross. She's one of our most promising and popular young professors. I hope that the two of you will become better acquainted in the next few weeks." The professor favored them with a congenial smile.

"We've already had a very memorable introduction," Ross replied, barely hiding his surprise at the professor's words. "I must admit I didn't realize this morning that Marnie and I have so much in common, but perhaps it's just as well we didn't waste too much time talking. Actions do speak louder than words sometimes." His smug double entendre caused Marnie's nerves to bristle.

"They say that water seeks its own level, Mr. Landry," she replied bitingly. "Or is the expression birds of a feather flock together? But then I would have supposed that big-time operators like yourself would disdain association with petty horse thieves like me. 'Borrowing' museum artifacts must be so much more rewarding than horseflesh." She noted with satisfaction the grim tightening of his jaw as he gave her an icy glare. She had managed to stir up the gravel once again.

The professor's throaty chuckle broke the deafening silence. "I see now why you invited me along tonight to referee, my dear. But I'll warn both of you right now, there'll be no more hitting below the belt this round! I insist on civilized conversation at the dinner table. Now let's continue over a bottle of retsina. It will soothe everyone's nerves."

Marnie bit her lip with consternation as she listened to the two men chat on their way to the dining room. It was apparent that they had known each other for years. With a sense of chagrin, she realized that the professor was going to be very little help, after all. It was up to her to tackle Ross's insufferable ego.

To everyone's relief, the professor's prediction about the effects of retsina were correct. His efforts at restoring harmony gained momentum as Ross's velvet charm resurfaced. Even Marnie found herself joining in the temporary truce. Gradually the tension at the table relaxed into polite congeniality. Although she often felt Ross's gaze studying her, by the end of the main course, Marnie was actually beginning to enjoy the evening.

The last two hours had been very instructive, she reflected as the waiter removed the remains of the savory grilled lamb and stuffed grape leaves from their table. Ross's conversation with the professor had indicated that he was a longtime benefactor of the university's archaeology department. Yet she knew that some of the top institutions in the country had disdained association with him since the scandal. She was troubled by the thought that perhaps the professor's attitude toward Ross was colored by the size of the grants he made to the university. Could a budget-conscious department chairman afford to snub large checks, even if they were endorsed by a suspected thief? Money talks, Marnie conceded ruefully. Fortunately, there were still some things that it wouldn't buy. She silently vowed that Ross would find it difficult to purchase her good will.

Although her plan for revenge had been thwarted,

she was satisfied with the fact that she had spoiled Ross's intentions for a seductive dinner. His high-handed bargain had fallen flat. At the very least, the contest should be ruled a draw. She was content with that outcome; slanting him a glance, she wondered if he was too.

As their waiter finished clearing the table, Ross excused himself to speak to someone at the bar. Marnie and the professor were left alone to linger over piping hot coffee and honey-drenched pastry. With a sigh of contentment, she smiled at him from across the table.

"Thank you for your patience, Professor. You've turned the evening into a pleasant experience."

"And you were sure that it wouldn't be." Professor Harte chuckled wryly, his blue eyes twinkling. "I guess I'm one of the few archaeologists around who doesn't think that Ross is some kind of two-faced monster. But I never did believe that cock-and-bull story that was splashed all over the news." He reached for another pastry. "Ross has told me that he did nothing wrong. I choose to believe him rather than that garbage in the newspapers."

"You have a lot of faith in him, Professor," Marnie commented quietly, stirring cream into her coffee.

"I've known Ross since he was a boy, and I trust my instincts," the professor responded. "I realize there are scholars who won't accept grants from him anymore because of Atlantis, but I think that's ridiculous. Ross wasn't convicted of any crime. There are very few universities around who can afford to examine all their sponsors under a magnifying glass; they'd be shocked at the outcome if they did."

"But what about the allegations that he stole muse-um artifacts?" she persisted. "How can you ignore that?"

"No one has proven that Ross stole anything," he

replied. "I suspect that the real facts of the case have been blown way out of proportion. I promise you that Ross is not a thief."

"What is he doing in Crete?" Marnie asked, sipping the strong Greek coffee with a contemplative expression.

"Ross established this dig. Every summer he spends a few weeks working with his research team here. He foots all of the expenses, and he even bought and refurbished this hotel for their convenience. The entire left wing is reserved for researchers and their families."

"You make him sound like an archaeologist's dream," she responded dryly.

"I admit that he can be the very devil when he wants something badly enough." The professor smiled. "There's no telling him 'no' sometimes. But his generosity to researchers is simply unequaled." He paused for a moment to regard her with a sober expression. "He's been good to our department, Marnie. No matter what you think of him personally, I wish you'd cultivate his friendship for that reason. We owe him a great deal."

Professor Harte's attention shifted as he noticed Ross motioning to him from across the room. "Excuse me a moment, my dear. I'll be right back."

Marnie stared thoughtfully at the professor as he walked away. The evening had certainly been full of surprises. She had to admit that the professor's confidence in Ross was difficult to ignore. Perhaps she had judged him too quickly. But the news stories she remembered reading about the scandal had been so damning. And Ross himself seemed so completely oblivious to any rules except his own. She instinctively knew that he was capable of simply seizing whatever he wanted from life and making it his own, without regard to other people's opinions. The questions remained in her mind: What did Ross Landry really want, and how far would he go to obtain it?

"Alone at last!" Ross's dramatic sigh brought Marnie to attention fast. He lowered his frame into the chair next to hers with the supple grace of a jungle cat.

"Where's the professor?" Her voice held a note of dawning suspicion. "He said he'd be right back."

"I'm afraid he's deserted us. He ran into an old friend at the bar whom he hasn't seen in years. He asked me to make his apologies to you." Ross watched her with a hawkish glint in his dark eyes.

"Then it's time I was leaving, too. Tomorrow will be a very busy day." Marnie reached for her bag.

"No, please don't go yet." His hand caught her arm lightly but firmly. "Let's go out on the terrace and have a nightcap. We should at least drink a toast to the dolphin's health." As he saw her hesitation, he pledged with an affable grin, "I promise to behave like a perfect gentleman."

Marnie wasn't sure if it was his words or his smile that swayed her. There was no denying his charm or persistence. Despite their misunderstandings, she was grateful to him for his help in rescuing the dolphin. It probably wouldn't have been possible without him, bargain or not. She owed him some courtesy at least. And the professor had requested that she make an effort to be cordial.

The bougainvillea-draped terrace was almost deserted as they seated themselves at a small, marble-topped table. The soft lights of the bar couldn't dim the brilliance of the stars above their heads. Jasmine scented the air. It was a perfect summer night.

Marnie was aware of Ross's probing eyes upon her as the waiter left with their order. Sensing a subtle change in his mood, she glanced quizzically across the table at his shadowed features.

"How can you look so serious on such a lovely evening?" Her eyes teased him gently. "We're celebrating the dolphin's successful rescue, remember? This is a happy occasion."

"But I've got serious matters on my mind," Ross replied, quirking his lips into a lazy smile. His mesmerizing gaze held hers for a long moment before he continued. "Tell me, Marnie, why did you invite the professor along this evening? Surely a woman of your accomplishments and independence doesn't always travel with a chaperon?" His voice was light, but she could sense more than idle curiosity behind the question.

"After our meeting this morning, can you blame me for seeking safety in numbers?" She deliberately kept her tone relaxed.

"Don't tell me that I frighten you?" Ross's inflection was mockingly hopeful.

"Not at all," she denied with a smile.

"Were you perhaps concerned that I might try to seduce you between courses?" He slanted an exaggerated leer in her direction.

"Don't be ridiculous," she scoffed. "Despite what you thought this morning, I'm not a lonely spinster looking for a vacation thrill." Just what had she done by agreeing to this drink? she wondered to herself.

"I hope you didn't think I might embarrass you by stealing the hotel's silver out from under the maître d's nose?" he inquired sardonically.

Marnie glared at him without comment. Belatedly, she realized that he was getting far too close to the mark.

"Correct me if I'm wrong, but I received the distinct impression this evening that you didn't expect the professor and me to be on speaking terms," he continued. "Am I right in thinking that your feelings had something to do with my alleged activities as a thief?"

Ross leaned forward in his chair to study her expression in the soft light. She could see that his brow was furrowed in determination. There would be no avoiding the question.

Suppressing a shiver of unease, she acknowledged to herself that his thinking was startlingly perceptive and his ability to read her mind disconcerting. She forced herself to meet the intensity of his gaze.

"You must admit that you've earned a rather unsavory reputation," she pointed out in a reasonable tone. "Everyone has read the news stories about you."

"I don't care about everyone's opinion," he answered gruffly. "What does interest me is the opinion in that beautiful blond head of yours. To be honest, I suspect that you hoped the professor and I would spend all evening at each other's throats. Meanwhile, you intended to watch from the sidelines and gleefully egg us on." His eyes gleamed with sparks of red and gold.

"It would have served you right, too," she retorted.

"Just as I thought," he said in disgust. He leaned back in his chair and fell silent, a stern, brooding expression covering his hawklike features.

Marnie glanced uncomfortably at him as she swirled the ouzo in the small glass in her hand. Perhaps she was being unfair, she thought with a touch of remorse. If the professor was right, she was being unjust to the department's most important benefactor. And Ross did look genuinely unhappy, sitting there staring out over the terrace wall. Her sense of fair play made her soften her tone.

"Look, I admit that I did recognize you this morning. And I had every intention of spoiling your smug plans for a seductive dinner date. After all, you did twist my arm rather forcefully," she chastised him.

"So you recognized me and naturally assumed the worst." The hint of gravel in his voice deepened.

"When you saw me with your horse, you assumed

the worst about me," she pointed out. "You thought I was a thief."

"But I caught you red-handed," he reminded her. "You, on the other hand, didn't catch me with evidence of any crime."

"Your picture was on the front page of every newspaper and magazine in the country. You can't expect people to ignore the accusations made against you!"

"I expect people not to convict me without the proper evidence!" He slammed his fist against the table for emphasis, rattling the glasses. "And I assure you that not a shred of proof was ever found to link me to the theft. The Greek government would never have allowed me to return if they had had the smallest doubt about my honesty." His dusky eyes held a sober expression. "I want you to believe that."

Their eyes met for a breathless moment. Marnie noted the sincerity in his proud demeanor. It seemed so important to him that she believe his innocence. Why shouldn't she take him at his word? she asked herself. He denied that he was guilty of the charges, and the professor supported his contention. American justice demanded that a man be considered innocent until proven guilty. What harm would it do if she accepted his assurances, if only for the sake of harmony in the next few weeks? Ross was obviously telling her the truth. She knew the Greek government enforced very strict standards on foreign researchers. If they had the least suspicion about him, he wouldn't have been allowed to enter Crete. It wasn't fair of her to condemn him without concrete proof.

"You're asking me to make up my own mind, to let you prove that you're innocent." A small smile curved her lips. Ross Landry was hardly the sort of man she would choose for an enemy under normal circumstances. Why ruin her first trip to Crete with ugly suspicions?

"I'd be disappointed if you didn't," he responded, a twitch of humor returning to his solemn face. "At least get to know me before you convict me. I hope we've got that settled. Truce?"

"Truce," she agreed with a nod.

They paused as the waiter returned with two more tiny glasses of ouzo. The clear syrupy liqueur clouded as he expertly added a few drops of water to their glasses. Ross motioned his thanks as the waiter bowed and left.

"To the dolphin." Marnie raised her glass in a toast.

"Who brought us together," Ross added, clinking his glass against hers. Their eyes met as each sipped the liqueur. She felt a surge of warmth suffuse her body that wasn't due entirely to the ouzo.

"I gather that you'll be working with the professor on one of his pet projects this summer." Ross smoothly shifted topics. "How did you ever manage to replace his faithful associate Bassett?"

Marnie smiled in spite of herself. The professor's longtime associate did rather resemble a mournful hound. "Roger Bass and his wife are relocating to Wisconsin. They needed some time to get settled in their new home, so he won't be coming for two to three weeks. I'm filling in until the end of June, then I'm returning to teach a summer seminar."

"I can see that I'm going to have to work quickly." Ross regarded her across the table with a speculative glint in his eyes. "This may have to be one of the fastest summer romances on record."

"A one-day acquaintance hardly qualifies as a romance," she replied in a firm voice. "Although I'm grateful to you for your help with the dolphin, I think we'd better concentrate on being friends this summer."

"Gratitude isn't exactly the emotion I had hoped to inspire." He sighed. "Did you honestly kiss me this morning simply out of gratitude?" Noting the color flushing her cheeks, he smiled. "I didn't think so either. But tell me why a romance is out of the question. Is there someone waiting at home?"

Placing her hands flat on the table in front of her, Marnie eyed him with steely resolve. She hadn't been involved with anyone in nearly three years, not since Rick had betrayed her trust. After that heartbreak, she had thrown herself into her studies, devoting all of her time to her graduate research. Gradually she had found fulfillment in her successful career. She wasn't about to let any man threaten her equilibrium now. Her cool poise asserted itself. She had to nip this in the bud before it went any further.

"We barely know each other. I'll only be here a short time and I have a great deal of work to do. I intend to spend my few spare hours sightseeing and soaking up the sun. I have no time for a relationship of any kind." Her green eyes met his gaze squarely.

Ross's vibrant chuckle echoed through the stillness of the night. "I'm on firmer ground than I'd dared hope. After only one day's acquaintance, as you termed it, I'm already regarded as a serious distraction to your work."

"You flatter yourself," Marnie responded coldly. Didn't his ego ever admit defeat?

"Why don't we try combining work with pleasure? It is possible," he assured her brightly, ignoring her glare. "For instance, only a short walk from here are the ruins of an ancient temple that you really must see. It will give you an excellent background in understanding our excavations at the dig. I'm a competent guide. Let's go!" He rose and motioned to the waiter.

"You mean now?" Marnie exclaimed, caught off guard. "But it's pitch black. We won't be able to see a thing."

"There's a full moon rising tonight," he promised. "And you haven't lived until you've seen Grecian ruins flooded with moonlight."

Despite the lateness of the hour and her better judgment, Marnie found herself agreeing to the jaunt. This was, after all, only her first full day in Crete, and the lure of moonlit ruins was irresistible to an archaeologist.

As Ross led the way up the darkened hillside, she forced herself to acknowledge that there was a certain chemistry between them. Although she could have had her pick of the eligible bachelors around the university, none of them, not even Rick, had ever affected her like Ross. His powerful masculinity drew her attention like a magnet and warmed her senses like a flame.

But her attraction to him made her doubly cautious. The life-styles of a college professor and a wealthy investment banker were worlds apart. And so too were their expectations about relationships, she reminded herself. While Ross sought a casual summer fling, she yearned for the intimacy of a more solid commitment. She had almost made a bitter mistake with Rick. And burned once, she was not willing to play with fire again. She had learned her lesson well.

The ruins were all he had promised, and more. The huge Doric columns looked as though they had been standing guard on this hilltop in Crete since the beginning of time. Silver moonbeams cast deep shadows against the crumbling marble, seeming to summon the ghosts of the temple's ancient worshippers to this small clearing. Marnie marveled at the overwhelming sense of eternity the scene depicted. This was the Greece of the all-powerful gods and goddesses, the mythical land of centaurs, nymphs and herculean heroes.

She felt Ross's hand at her waist as she stood

admiring the temple. Unconsciously, she relaxed against the comfort of his muscular arm. "Thank you for bringing me here, Ross. It's perfect." Her voice was almost a whisper; her eyes glowed with contentment. She had waited so long to view this magical country for herself. It was a dream come true.

"This temple was built to honor the god Neptune," he explained softly. "As a seafaring nation, the Greek people set great store in appeasing the mighty deity of the sea. In the daylight you can see that three sides of the structure face the Mediterranean. That way, they could make sure that Neptune wouldn't miss any of the festivities they had arranged in his honor."

"But I thought the early Cretans worshipped bulls as their gods," Marnie mused. "How did Neptune rate this temple?"

"It was built some time later than the palace that we're excavating at the dig," he responded. "The same foreign invaders who destroyed the Minoan civilization of the early Cretans probably built this temple for themselves."

"You're a knowledgeable guide." She smiled up at him.

"I told you," he murmured against her ear, "work and pleasure aren't mutually exclusive. Especially if you choose the right companion for your guide." His warm breath fanned her cheek as she felt her heart quicken its pace.

"Are you volunteering your services with no strings attached?" she inquired skeptically, trying to stem the warm tide of excitement spreading through her veins.

"I promise I can take you places that you've never dreamed of before, little mermaid. Don't you think a deed of that sort should be rewarded?" His voice was smoothly persuasive.

Marnie stiffened as his arms came around her shoulders. Moving abruptly to one side, she broke his light grasp. She had briefly lost control this morning when he had kissed her. That was one mistake she was determined not to repeat. It was vital that she escape his spell now while she was still able to, she told herself. Things were progressing much too fast between them. Her common sense cautioned prudence. She took a deep breath to steady her pounding heartbeat and turned to face him.

"What's wrong?" Ross dropped his arms slowly to his side. He made no attempt to follow her, but his dark eyes probed her face.

"I'm tired. I want to go back to the hotel now." Marnie hoped he would mistake the tremor in her voice for weariness. "I guess I'm still suffering from jet lag," she explained, dropping her eyes from his perceptive gaze.

She could sense Ross watching her through the darkness and she was glad that the moon had picked that moment to disappear behind a cloud. The only sounds were the faint lapping of the waves against the shore in the distance and the melodious trill of a nearby nightingale. They were alone on the hillside.

"I guess it has been a pretty exhausting day all around," he agreed softly. "I'm willing to cut the tour short on one condition: I want you to promise that from now on when we have dinner together you won't bring uninvited guests along." His baritone voice held a hint of reproach.

"I promise," Marnie answered, eager to end the evening. She longed to be alone in her room. Ross's ability to stir her senses was confusing and a little frightening. She was too tired to try and sort out her feelings tonight. She wanted only to escape.

"Good. I have to be in Iráklion all day tomorrow for a meeting at the museum, but I'll be back by seven. I'll pick you up then." He laid a finger gently against her lips to silence her protest. "We need time to get to know each other. I intend to see that we get it," he vowed.

Chapter Three

"Roger will take the photographs necessary to supplement our text when he arrives," the professor explained, flipping shut the spiral notebook he held in one hand. "Our editor has promised to use as many pictures of the site as possible, so I want to give her a well-rounded selection to choose from."

He paused, glancing at Marnie's intently bent head as he drained the last swallow of coffee from his cup. She nodded in silent agreement, her eyes never leaving the thick pad in front of her that she was covering with hasty notes. Her shorthand skills had been a real time-saver during her student days. Now she practiced just enough to keep from getting rusty.

A light breeze wafted in through the open French windows of the study where she and the professor were seated at one of the large oak tables. The shimmering heat of the noon sun had not yet penetrated the room's thick stucco walls. Away from the hotel's main traffic areas, the spartanly furnished study was hushed and conducive to quiet conversations.

"Why don't we include some line drawings of the site, Professor? Perhaps some before-and-after illustrations to emphasize the progress the research team has made," she suggested, narrowing her eyes thoughtfully.

"That would be fine," he agreed. "Ross has promised us complete access to his files here, and we can also request additional material from his Athens office. You're sure to find the information you need between those two sources." The professor waved his hand at the neat rows of books lining two walls of the study from ceiling to floor. "We can make use of his reference library as well."

At a glance, Marnie could see that the shelves contained virtually every major work concerning modern archaeology published in recent years. Current issues of scholarly journals were stacked along the bottom tier of one bookcase. Ross obviously spared no expense when it came to his library.

"I talked to his assistant this morning, Professor, and he promised to go through the files with me tomorrow."

"Good! Paul will be a great help to us, I'm sure. He knows those files backwards and forwards. Pull out anything you find that pertains to the choice of this site and its early development. That's what we'll focus on in the first article. I'd like to see the organization of this dig serve as a model for other researchers."

Marnie regarded him with a thoughtful expression. "They were certain that this was the exact site of the palace long before any digging began, weren't they?"

"As certain as humanly possible." He nodded. "Ross even commissioned detailed drawings of what the structures and grounds probably looked like based on the excavations of similar palaces at Knossos and Phaestos."

"Did the drawings include a labyrinth for the royal family's Minotaur?" Marnie couldn't suppress a smile as she thought of the mythical Cretan beast fabled to possess the head of a bull and the body of a man. Legend held that the monster was the result of a shameful mating between a Cretan queen and an albino bull.

"Anything is possible, especially on Crete," the professor acknowledged, his eyes twinkling humorously. "Even though the Minoan civilization of early Crete was relatively sophisticated for its time, the people attributed strange powers to bulls. Custom decreed that the Minotaur's lust could only be satisfied by the yearly sacrifice of seven beautiful maidens."

"In that case, I think I ran into one of his bullheaded descendants on the beach yesterday," she commented dryly.

"Well, I've heard Ross described in less flattering terms, my dear, but never by a woman. I do hope that the two of you cleared the air last night?" He regarded her with a curious glance over the top of his glasses.

"We've agreed to a truce of sorts," she admitted, recalling her conversation with Ross on the terrace. She arched a delicate eyebrow pointedly in the professor's direction. "I'm sorry you had to eat and run last night, Professor. Ross mentioned that you ran into an old friend." Her voice was laced with a hint of saccharine sweetness.

"You understand how those things happen sometimes," he mumbled, looking uncomfortable. "Let's break for lunch and then spend the afternoon at the dig getting our bearings."

The next few hours flew by as Marnie examined the dig for the first time. She knew that the ancient Cretans had been called Minoans after one of their early kings, and that their palaces had housed the entire courts of the local princes. As she and the professor entered the site, he pointed out the remnants of the ornamental western façade of the palace, telling her that entrance to the grounds had generally been through more modest gates a few yards away. From there, twisted paths had led into the central courtyard, which had been a rectangular space approximately one hundred and fifty feet by eighty feet.

Marnie and the professor worked their way around the site, discussing ideas and jotting down notes. They paused frequently to talk to the dozen or more archaeologists at work under the blazing sun with trowels, penknives and brushes. The researchers showed them the crumbled foundations of storerooms and houses that they had already unearthed north of the main courtyard. Marnie learned that most of the excavation efforts this summer would focus on the area to the south where they hoped to uncover the palace's throne room.

She found herself listening to the archaeologists' enthusiastic plans for the summer with rapt attention. Despite the bad publicity generated by the Atlantis scandal, Ross had assembled an impressive group of professionals for this project. She couldn't ignore the fact that they all appeared to have enormous confidence and respect for him. It was apparently an all-or-nothing situation, she reflected. People either hated Ross or they sang his praises. There seemed to be no middle ground.

The sun had dipped below the crest of the rugged hillside before she headed back to the hotel. A hasty glance at her watch told her that she just had time for a short bath if she was to meet Ross at seven. Although she had been reluctant to agree to this dinner date at first, she now felt poised and in control. She had even jotted down a list of subjects to quiz him on; after all, who could answer her questions about the dig better than the mastermind of the operation himself?

The sweetly cloying fragrance of jasmine greeted her senses as she crossed the threshold of her room. Her attention was instantly drawn to the delicate sprigs of yellow flowers filling a crystal vase on her dresser. The waxy blossoms looked as though they had just been plucked from the bush moments ago.

She reached for the white note tucked among the glossy leaves. "These reminded me of you, sweet lady. . . . Dress is casual tonight—we dine among the natives." Marnie smiled as she deciphered the scrawling *R* at the bottom. Whatever his other faults, charm was not one of Ross's shortcomings. The velvet side of his personality could be devastating to a woman's will, as she was learning fast. Fortunately, now that she had sampled its danger, she knew how to protect herself from its potent spell.

Humming a cheerful tune, she peeled off her dusty jeans and tailored plaid shirt. As she ran the water for her bath, she swept her hair into a loose bun, securing it to the top of her head with a scarf. She slipped into the lemon-scented bubbles with a sigh of contentment and stretched back to allow the water to work its magic on her muscles. Minutes later she emerged, refreshed and relaxed.

Heeding Ross's suggestion about casual attire, she chose a simple linen sundress from her closet. The rich rose color of the natural fabric had always been one of her favorites; the scooped neckline and sleeveless bodice displayed her recently acquired tan to good advantage. The dress was as cool and comfortable as it was flattering to her slender figure.

She brushed her hair until it floated around her shoulders in a silken halo. Eyeing herself critically in the mirror, she decided to leave her hair loose tonight. After all, Ross had specified casualness.

The marble lobby appeared deserted as she descended the stairway. Wide doors leading onto the terrace stood open, flooding the room with the rainbow rays of the setting sun. A ceiling fan swung its mahogony blades lazily, circulating the cool evening air as it emerged from the shadows. In one corner of the room, potted palms rustled softly. The air was heavy with the scent of jasmine.

There was no sign of Ross, but Marnie did see Dale Stover, one of the researchers she had met that afternoon, lounging against the arm of a rattan sofa. The tall, blond Californian looked very much at home in his tennis whites and expensive sneakers. Bronzed and athletic, he seemed impatient to be out on the clay courts adjoining the back of the hotel.

Dale saluted her with a leisurely wave of the metal racket he held in one hand. Marnie smiled in his direction. The high heels of her Italian sandals tapped a staccato echo against the polished marble floor as she walked over to chat with him.

"You look like an exotic blossom in that dress, Marnie," he greeted her with a bold, admiring stare. "You must have a big evening planned."

"Not really." She perched on the edge of a chair across from him. "Just dinner in the village. You look eager for a match," she added, ignoring his wolfish gaze.

"I'm supposed to play singles with Jerry Burke, but he's late." Dale glanced at the elegant Swiss watch on his wrist. "It's almost seven-fifteen." His cultured voice sounded faintly petulant.

As he turned his head once again toward the stairway, Marnie saw his eyes narrow to tiny slits. She was startled by the hostility that flashed across his refined features. For a second, his lips curled in spite, then a mask of feigned indifference cloaked his face.

Following the direction of his gaze, she saw Ross striding across the lobby toward them. He was dressed in tailored black trousers and a pearl-gray silk shirt that hugged his lean frame. His sleeves were rolled back, exposing the long, sinewy muscles of his forearms. Marnie felt her pulse quicken at the sight of him.

But Ross hardly spared her a glance, his gaze glued instead to Dale's impassive face. As he drew nearer, she recognized the hard expression that shadowed his features. Looking from Ross back to Dale, she realized that a confrontation of some sort was imminent. It was obvious that these two men were adversaries.

Ross halted behind Marnie's chair, his frosty gaze never seeming to leave Dale's. She felt his hands lower to rest against her shoulders, pressing her back against the brightly printed cushions of the chair in a possessive gesture. Marnie suddenly felt as though she had been trapped in a cage between two feuding panthers.

"What are you doing here?" Ross's blunt demand sliced through the dense air above her head. Tension hung like a black fog between the two men. She felt an uneasy flutter of apprehension in her stomach.

"Now, now. That's no way to welcome your cousin to Crete," Dale chided in a patronizing tone. "But then I guess some people never learn any manners." His sky-blue eyes regarded Ross with a mixture of arrogance and distaste.

"Some people insist on poking their noses where they aren't wanted," Ross countered. "Jerry tells me that you suddenly showed up here out of the blue several days ago. I want to know why you've come." His tone brooked no nonsense.

Dale sighed elaborately, as if placating an unreasonable child. "Father intended to be here next week, as you know, but something came up, and he's going to be delayed. With you in Geneva and Professor Davenport ill, he was afraid the team would be shorthanded. He asked me to come in his place and lend a hand. I was delighted, of course, for the chance to work once again with your illustrious research group." Dale smirked at Ross as if daring him to object.

Marnie felt Ross's hands momentarily tighten their grip on her shoulders. The blatant hostility between the men made her feel uncomfortable and awkward, but she didn't dare move from the chair. Ross's strong fingers held her pinned to the spot.

"Your contributions to this group have been more than ample," Ross asserted with a touch of bitterness in his voice. "Uncle Charles was mistaken. I'm back, and the team is not shorthanded. We don't want your help."

"It's really not so bad, dear cousin," Dale pointed out in a snide tone. "I only promised to stay until Father arrives, then I'm off to Cannes. I wouldn't dream of staying long enough to wear out my welcome."

"Maybe I haven't made myself clear," Ross gritted through clenched teeth. "You're not welcome here—period."

Although she couldn't see his face, Marnie knew by the tone of Ross's voice that his temper was nearing the boiling point. He sounded as though he wanted to strangle Dale right then and there. She couldn't help but wonder at the cause of such enmity between cousins.

"Of course, Father couldn't have known that you had extra help lined up." Dale's gaze raked insolently across Marnie. "But tell me, how are you going to explain your latest conquest to Sandra when she arrives?"

"Leave Marnie and Sandra out of this," Ross grated with barely suppressed fury. "I want you out of here by tomorrow afternoon—sooner if possible!"

"Are you going to explain to Father why I'm not here?" Dale snapped. "He won't be pleased."

"I'll handle Uncle Charles when the time comes. All you have to do is pack up and leave." Ross's tone threatened with deadly aim. "If you don't, he's going to learn some very disturbing facts about his only son."

Dale rose, looking deflated. "If the two of you will excuse me, I've got a tennis partner to chase down. I'm sorry we won't get the opportunity to continue our chat, Marnie. I'd be delighted to enlighten you further about your escort's nasty temper . . . Ciao."

"Ciao . . ." Marnie echoed as he strode away in the direction of the tennis courts. She stared after him as if he held the key to a mystery that troubled her. If only she had a clue to help her unravel the scene she had just witnessed. She sensed that it might be important in helping her understand the enigmatic man who stood as stiff as a statue behind her.

Shifting slightly in her chair, Marnie tilted her head up to glance at Ross's chiseled profile. There was a grim set to his jaw. His smoky eyes were unfathomable as he turned to look down at her.

"My cousin has a real knack for spoiling my appetite," he remarked bitterly.

"Why don't we postpone having dinner in the village tonight?" she suggested. Whatever the cause of the animosity between the two men, it had clearly upset Ross more than she would have imagined. An evening on the town seemed out of place now.

"No!" Ross's response was fast and furious. Before Marnie could protest, he pulled her out of the chair and swung her around to face him. "We're having dinner tonight as we planned. Just the two of us!" Not waiting for a reply, he propelled her out of the lobby and down the steps to the side of the hotel where he had parked his car.

She flashed an admiring glance at the elegant yet sporty Mercedes convertible sparkling sassily beside the curb. Its gleaming silver metal looked spotless despite the dusty Greek roads. The black top was tucked snuggly behind the seats, leaving the plush gray interior open to the sky. Ross helped her into the passenger's seat with a brusque motion and slammed the door as if to prevent her escape.

Marnie leaned back against the soft leather seat and studied him from the corner of her eye as he slipped behind the wheel. His face was as tense as a coiled spring. Turning the key in the ignition, he gunned the engine, and the sleek automobile accelerated as if it had wings. She clutched the armrest, silently wondering when his temper would blow. The idea of riding around with all that anger pent up behind the wheel wasn't very reassuring.

"Look, I'd really prefer not to go out tonight if you don't feel . . ." she began, raising her voice slightly to be heard above the purr of the engine.

"What were you and Dale talking about before I arrived?" The harshness of Ross's tone sliced across her words. "Was my charming cousin filling your head with his self-serving lies?"

"Lies about what?" Marnie faced him with a perplexed frown. The fact that Ross disliked his cousin was obvious, but now he sounded furious with her, too. Why would her innocent chat with Dale arouse such anger? What was eating him?

"There's no limit to Dale's resourcefulness, but I suspect that I'm still the favorite target of his forked tongue." He spat out the words without a glance in her direction. His eyes were cemented to the road.

"Your name didn't even enter the conversation," she pointed out stiffly, beginning to lose patience with him.

"Then why do you keep insisting that we not go out this evening?" His accusation stung the air like a whip. "Dale is a troublemaker. Don't believe anything he told you. And stay away from him in the future!"

"What gives you the right to think you can choose my friends?" Incensed by his domineering attitude, she thinned her lips into an angry line. She wasn't going to allow him to get away with such high-handed behavior. He was taking far too much for granted where she was concerned.

Ross jammed his foot hard on the brake pedal, the tires screeching their protest against the hot pavement. The back end of the Mercedes fishtailed before he brought the vehicle to a stop and switched off the engine.

"This gives me the right!" He reached across the seat to grasp her wrists with his strong hands. Pulling her forcefully into his arms, he laced his fingers through the hair at the nape of her neck and tilted her mouth up to meet his. She caught only a glimpse of the molten fire in his eyes before his lips claimed hers.

Ross's mouth was harsh, with only a whisper of the tenderness he had shown in the cove. His lips ravished her soft mouth as if he were trying to drive every thought from her mind except the primitive hunger of desire. The kiss demanded her complete submission to his masculine will.

Marnie fought to restrain her awakening response to him, but her rebellious body refused to obey. Her slim frame molded itself against his granite strength, and her lips parted to welcome his probing tongue. She moaned as his assault on her mouth continued, each thrust of his tongue inciting her to respond with a growing wave of excitement. A surge of heat kindled in her veins, aroused by the mastery of his touch.

But as his hand slipped down to stroke the swelling curve of her breast, a tiny alarm went off in her head. She felt a flashing resurgence of anger at his overbearing, arrogant behavior. She was accustomed to keeping men at a safe distance, ruled by a cool head and a firm hand. Ross's ability to break through her defenses was unprecedented, but that didn't entitle him to any liberties where she was concerned.

Slowly his lips softened as he felt her withdrawal from him. Then, as suddenly as he began, he stopped, raising his head to study her with the probing force of his gaze.

Marnie's green eyes burned with resentment as she stared up at him. "I think you'd better understand that you have no rights over me at all." Her voice was deadly calm. He still held her an unwilling prisoner to his sinewy strength, but she was determined to fight back the only way she knew how: with cold, hard reason.

"I can't begin to fathom the hostility between you and Dale," she continued. "But I'm not going to allow you to take your anger out on me. I've done nothing to deserve it."

Ross stared at her for a long moment before answering. "You're right. I guess I lost my head." Releasing her arms, he raked his fingers through his rumpled hair in a gesture of frustration. "When you seemed so willing to forgo our dinner plans, I thought that Dale had tried to poison you against me. He's not above that kind of thing." His dusky eyes searched hers. "I was afraid that you might be retreating from the truce we made last night. I don't want you to do that."

Marnie stifled the absurd impulse to reach out and smooth his hair. It seemed ridiculous to want to comfort someone who had just deliberately tried to hurt her, but Ross looked genuinely contrite. Instead, she asked in a quiet voice, "Why does Dale hate you so?"

Expelling a heavy sigh, he stared out through the windshield at the darkening twilight. "Dale and I have never been close. There's always been a strong degree of competition between us. A few months after I took over my father's company, I discovered Dale acting against the best interests of the firm during a key merger deal. I warned him then that if he ever did it again, cousin or not, he was through." Ross paused pensively.

"And he ignored your warning," she guessed, resting her head against the leather upholstery. Her eyes watched the mixture of emotions flitting across Ross's face.

"My father had given Dale a position in the company as a favor to Uncle Charles. I suppose Dale thought that I wouldn't go against one of my father's last wishes, but he was wrong. I was solely responsible for the welfare of the company by then, and I fired him."

"Is Dale an archaeologist, too?" The thin line of a frown marred Marnie's smooth brow.

"No, but my uncle is, as well as being the director of the Landry foundation. Dale grew up around digs and museums, so he knows the basics. Unfortunately, he's never settled down long enough to really develop any career. He's more than satisfied with living off his trust funds and jetting around the globe at a moment's notice."

"Not to mention showing up to aggravate you," she pointed out with a twitch of humor.

"Yes," he admitted with a grimace. "He's been a thorn in my side ever since Father died. But look, why don't we start the evening all over again? Let's forget that scene in the lobby ever happened." There was a pleading note in his husky baritone that she couldn't ignore.

"I'll agree on one condition." Marnie smiled, mimicking the bargaining tone he had used with her in the cove. "There's no such thing as a free lunch—as you so aptly reminded me yesterday—but I do have some questions about the dig that need answers. Now if you're willing to supply me with information, I'm willing to start the evening again." Her green eyes sparkled with a devilish light.

Groaning in submission, he nodded. "Okay, you win. It's a deal, but I have the feeling I'm going to regret teaching you the finer points of bargaining." Leaning toward her, he sealed the agreement with a light butterfly kiss on her lips. "I'm afraid I damaged your lipstick," he added ruefully.

By the time she had repaired her smeared lipstick and smoothed her hair, they were pulling up in front of a neatly whitewashed restaurant. One whiff of the tantalizing aromas wafting from the open-air terrace reminded Marnie that she had eaten only a salad for lunch.

"The food here is superb," Ross assured her, his mood mellowing. "We'll be invited to visit the kitchen, just as the villagers do, and choose our meal by sight and smell."

Marnie was delighted to find that he was right. They were greeted at the door by the proprietor, a portly giant who was squeezed into a spotless white apron several sizes too small for him. After exchanging several animated words in Greek with Ross, he escorted them to the kitchen with a beaming smile of hospitality lighting his swarthy face. Two female cooks busy chopping vegetables at a large butcher-block table also greeted them with smiles.

Marnie savored the array of steaming kettles and pots that were opened for her inspection. Ross watched her with amusement as he translated the contents of each dish. One cook led them over to a refrigerator where she proudly displayed the fresh fish and shrimp caught that morning by the local fishermen. They finally settled on a meal of charcoal-grilled mullet and eggplant moussaka. With a warm smile, Marnie thanked the cooks and the proprietor for their graciousness.

They found a table in a quiet corner of the vine-draped terrace forming the back of the restaurant. A solicitous waiter brought them plates of crisp salad dotted with the plump black olives and chunks of feta cheese considered the staples of the Cretan diet. A basket of piping hot yeast bread accompanied the herb-seasoned salads. At Ross's request, the waiter returned seconds later with a chilled bottle of retsina and two glasses.

Marnie felt Ross's smoky gaze studying her as she attacked her salad with gusto. "What have you been doing today to build such an appetite?" he teased her. "Last night you barely picked at your meal."

"I had a terrific day," she assured him. "The professor and I toured the dig this afternoon and talked with the researchers. My experience with field work has been rather limited until now, but I know that I'm going to love every minute of it."

An indulgent smile curved Ross's lips. "There's nothing like your first real field project," he agreed. "When I was sixteen, my father sent me to Italy for the summer where I worked at a dig under the watchful tutelage of Professor Harte. I sifted through the ruins of an ancient amphitheater in the stifling Italian heat just like a child with a new toy. I returned convinced that I should pursue archaeology as a full-time career. No stuffy bank presidency for me," he reminisced with a thoughtful expression.

Marnie's eyes widened in surprise. "What made you change your mind?"

He crooked an ironic smile at her, his dark eyes growing more serious. "Fate interrupted my plans. I had just completed graduate school when my father was killed in a small-plane crash. As the oldest son, I felt responsible for the future of the family banking interests. Although my father had given his full support to my studies, I knew that he would have preferred me to join him in the business. As it was, he had to look to my younger brothers to follow in his footsteps, and they were both still in high school when he died." Ross paused to sip some wine from his glass. "The only way I could protect their heritage for them was to put aside my career as an archaeologist and concentrate on mastering the field of investment banking."

"Is that why your foundation offers such generous funding to researchers?" she asked quietly. "Is it a compensation for the time you can't spend yourself?"

"I can't think of a better way to utilize my financial resources," he explained simply. "Now that my brothers are experienced enough to shoulder most of the business responsibilities, I'm able to slip away to the dig for a few weeks at a time just to keep my hand in an active project. Later this year I hope to be able to devote some time to reopening the Atlantis excavation. By then, I'll be functioning merely as a consultant for my family's banking interests."

Marnie studied his hawklike profile as he refilled their glasses with retsina. It seemed that a few media cranks had done an injustice to Ross in portraying him to the world as a dilettante who dabbled in archaeology only for amusement and profit. He was obviously a devoted professional. It must have been a wrenching experience to be forced to give up a career you had spent years studying for, only to start all over again in another field.

No wonder he had been so irritated with her yesterday when she had taunted him with the theft of the Atlantis artifacts. As a professional, the idea of dealing in black-market antiquities was probably as abhorrent to him as it was to her. She wondered how he had ever gotten mixed up in such a scandal. There were still so many unanswered questions about his past. She longed to discuss Atlantis with him, but she disliked the thought of stirring up his anger again. One display of temper in an evening was more than enough for her.

"A penny for your thoughts?" His mellow tone drew her back from her reverie.

Blushing a little under the intensity of his gaze, she reached for the small notebook she had tucked into her purse. "I think it's time I collected on our bargain," she replied.

"I've got all evening," he assured her with a grin. "Fire away."

By the time they finished a leisurely dinner followed by cups of strong black coffee, Marnie had made significant headway in accumulating background material for the article. Despite the limited amount of time Ross could devote to the dig, she found that he was knowledgeable and well informed about every part of the operation. She had to admit that she enjoyed the professional rapport that sprang up between them during the course of the discussion. It was hard not to admire a colleague who possessed so much enthusiasm for his work.

As they rose to leave, she realized that she had been so wrapped up in their conversation that she hadn't even noticed that most of the other patrons had already left the restaurant. Only one other couple still lingered over coffee while the white-aproned waiters bustled about finishing their evening chores.

Marnie felt Ross's hand at her waist as he guided her out of the restaurant and down a narrow street toward the lights of a small taverna. The distinctive twang of a bouzouki rippled through the night air as they neared the entrance.

"I thought we might have a nightcap here and dance awhile, if you like," he suggested.

At her nod of agreement, he led her through the open door and motioned to a waiter who escorted them to a table. The crowd seemed to consist mainly of young couples who were chatting together in groups or listening to the band that was warming up in the corner. The flickering candlelight on each table reflected the gaiety and good spirits lighting the swarthy faces of the simple village people surrounding them.

"The band here plays a good mixture of Greek and pop music," Ross explained over the noise of the instruments. "The young people here have adopted the western styles of dancing wholeheartedly. We'll take in some authentic traditional dancing some other evening. Tonight I just want to dance with you." His eyes flicked over her with a flamelike brilliance burning in their depths.

Marnie felt her heart do a silly flip-flop as she followed Ross to the dance floor. She had known him such a short time, yet just the touch of his hand or the warmth of his smile was enough to make her glow from head to toe. It was impossible to be near him and not feel bewitched by his velvet charm. Although she was reluctant to admit it, he was the only man who had ever made her feel this way.

She felt a growing surge of excitement warm her veins as Ross drew her to him. She moved easily into his arms as if she were accustomed to being there. Cradled against his solid frame, she swayed gracefully in time to the band's slow beat. His fingers wove their way through the silken strands of her hair to the back of her neck where they began a soothing, sensual massage. Marnie relaxed against him with a sigh of contentment.

"You feel as though you were made for my arms, little mermaid." His husky voice sounded close to her ear.

"That sounds just a trifle chauvinistic," she pointed out, tilting her head up to gaze at him. "You wouldn't by any chance subscribe to the outdated idea that women were made solely for the enjoyment of men, would you?" Her emerald eyes gleamed with a teasing challenge.

"I'll have you know that I resent being labeled an outdated chauvinist of any kind," he declared in a mock serious tone. "I actually hold very modern views on the subject. Men and women were made for each other's mutual and equal enjoyment." The intensity of his gaze mesmerized her, sending a quiver of anticipation tingling through her senses.

"And if we weren't surrounded by people," he continued, his warm breath caressing her cheek, "I'd prove it to you."

"If I weren't such an old-fashioned girl at heart, I just might let you try," she replied with total candor, gazing boldly into his dark eyes.

"I delight in an old-fashioned challenge, my dear," he promised with a determined smile. "And I must warn you that I can be a most persistent suitor."

He pulled her more tightly against him, molding his muscular arms around her slender body. Resting her head on his shoulder, Marnie could feel the throb of his heartbeat through the thin silk of his shirt.

He seems so sure of himself, she thought. So sure that a summer fling was exactly what he wanted. Instinctively she knew that an affair would never be enough for her. She couldn't let him ensnare her in that treacherous net; it would be a mistake she would always regret.

On the other hand, their life-styles were far too different for her to cherish daydreams that Ross might be seriously interested in her. It simply wasn't possible; they came from two different worlds. She would be a fool to imagine herself becoming emotionally involved with a man like Ross Landry. It wasn't the sensible thing to do, and she had always been painstakingly sensible.

It was past midnight by the time they left the taverna. The evening air gently caressed their faces as they sped back to the hotel. Marnie relaxed against the leather seat, the purr of the engine soon lulling her to sleep.

She awoke to the feel of Ross's lips brushing lightly yet insistently against hers. Responding to his kiss without thinking, she twined her arms around his neck and arched her body toward him. His hungry lips pressed against hers, igniting her senses with a rush of pleasure.

Suddenly he lifted his head to stare down at her in the dim light reflected from the entrance to the hotel. Opening her eyes, Marnie gazed at his face, trying to fathom the conflicting expressions that flitted across his chiseled features. For a moment, she thought she was still dreaming.

"You're enough to make any man forget his honorable intentions, little mermaid." He sighed in consternation. Reaching across her, he pushed open her door. "Inside with you now, before we both change our minds."

Marnie didn't need a second warning. As Ross drove off to park the car, she hastened across the lobby and up the stairs to the safety of her room. What could she have been thinking of? To respond so wantonly to his advances was inexcusable, regardless of the fact that she had been half asleep. She felt as though she had narrowly missed walking off a ledge into thin air. She was back on solid ground again and she felt secure . . . but strangely empty.

Chapter Four

The brilliant sunshine flooding in through the sliding glass doors of the balcony tugged Marnie awake. Narrowing her eyes against the intrusion, she yawned, stretching lazily. A casual glance at her watch pulled her out of bed with a lunge. She had overslept by a full hour!

That's what happens when you keep such late hours, she chastised herself as she adjusted the shower spray. A smile softened her lips as she thought back over her evening with Ross. She could almost feel his strong arms holding her close while they danced. Just the memory of his smoky eyes gazing down at her quickened the pace of her heart. Sighing deeply, she forced her attention back to the spurting water. There wasn't time to spend all morning daydreaming, she had work to do.

Slipping out of her lacy nightgown, she stepped under the tepid spray. Her mind spun in a thousand directions as she tried to plan her activities for the day. First, there was the appointment with Paul. Going over the dig's files would probably require most of the morning. Then she had the background research on early Crete to finish, and she wanted to spend some more time at the dig this afternoon. Ross had suggested that they meet for a swim in the cove before dinner. Were there enough hours in the day? she wondered happily.

Minutes later, dressed in tan jeans and a thin cotton shirt, she was ready to go. Grabbing her canvas tote and a fresh notebook, she headed for the door. For the first time she spied the square of folded paper lying just under the door. Frowning, she bent to pick it up. She hoped that Paul hadn't changed their plans.

Scanning the note quickly, she relaxed leaning back against the door. Ross's bold script was unmistakable. "Good morning, sleepyhead. I'll be waiting for you at the cove around six. I can't wait to see you in that bikini again!"

He certainly had a charming way of telling a woman how to dress. She grinned. She was lucky that whirlwind romances just weren't her style, otherwise she might be in some danger of succumbing to his allure. But she had learned to lead with her head rather than her emotions. Relationships were so much safer that way.

Her appointment with Paul yielded pages of useful information for her growing research file. The mild-mannered, scholarly young man was meticulous and organized, putting facts at her fingertips with an efficiency that delighted Marnie's own methodical instincts. Ross had equipped himself with a model assistant she decided as she watched the slim, red-haired Paul in action.

"That's everything through last summer," he told her at midmorning as they came to the end of a particularly voluminous file. "Why don't we stop for coffee? I'm sure we can finish the rest before lunch."

"Coffee sounds terrific," Marnie agreed. "I feel as though I've just whizzed through the last two and a half years of the dig's history. It's a rather heady experience."

"Most of our work for the first year consisted of sifting through tons of topsoil until we reached the layer on which the Minoans constructed their palace." Paul smiled, stretching back in his chair. "Some of the most interesting artifacts have just been uncovered in the last six months. A few of the pieces are in Ross's office. Would you like to see them now?"

"I'd love to," Marnie responded with an eager nod.

Paul led the way out of his office and down the hall to Ross's suite. Unlocking the door, he flicked on the overhead lights and gestured for Marnie to precede him into the outer office. Two long tables had been pushed together in an L-shape underneath the row of windows. An array of pottery fragments, sculpture, jewelry and seals were spread across the tabletops with museumlike orderliness.

Delighted, Marnie headed straight for the collection of miniature sculpture. "Professor Harte has been raving about the snake goddess that was found last week. I've been anxious to see her for myself."

"We're very proud of her." Paul smiled, enjoying Marnie's enthusiasm. "Minoan artists didn't create very much large-scale sculpture, but the craftsmanship they lavished on small pieces like this render them amazingly realistic."

"She is wonderful," Marnie exclaimed, bending over the delicate figure that was just large enough to fit in the palm of her hand. The tiny goddess stood in regal splendor, her arms spread wide to offer two writhing snakes toward the heavens. Typically Minoan, the woman wore a flounced skirt with a tight belt circling her waistline. Her shoulders and chest were bare except for a third snake coiled loosely around her throat like a necklace. The minute detail and lifelike expression etched into the clay made the goddess a timeless example of the richness and vitality of the Minoan culture.

"She deserves to be on exhibit in a museum," Marnie observed, her eyes glued to the goddess in fascination.

"She'll soon be on her way to one in Iráklion," Paul answered. "We were so excited about finding her that Ross called the curator himself with the news. I don't think our research team has been so elated about a single artifact since we found the ram's horn drinking cup during the Atlantis project."

"But weren't the Atlantis artifacts stolen from a museum?" Marnie asked, slanting a sharp glance at Paul.

"The drinking cup and other articles we found during Atlantis were uncovered by our own divers," he replied with a stern tightening of his jaw. "I was with the team all summer, and the articles the authorities identified as being stolen were not a part of our original collection. Many people have overlooked the fact that most of the relics we turned over to the museum were genuine."

"But where did the stolen items come from then?" she asked, gazing thoughtfully at the display of jewelry and seals.

"I don't know," Paul admitted, raking his fingers through his hair. "I did all the cataloging that summer and I'm certain that those items were not in the crates we sent to Athens. The first time I saw the stolen artifacts was in a newspaper photo weeks later."

"Didn't Ross confront the police with your story?"

"By then nobody wanted to listen. The whole thing had snowballed out of proportion, and the damage had been done. We moved on to other projects, and the publicity gradually ran its course." He shrugged as if it didn't matter anymore. "Atlantis is ancient history now."

"But the scandal must have crippled your team's credibility as professional researchers. Didn't anyone try to vindicate you?" she asked.

"Ross decided to accept full responsibility for the stolen artifacts himself in order to prevent the foundation from losing face. He even turned the position of director over to his uncle," Paul explained. "Since then, Ross has stayed in the background of all our research projects. His reputation has suffered far more than the foundation's, but I guess he's satisfied that he made the best of an impossible situation."

"I see," Marnie responded softly. Ross's behavior seemed incomprehensible to her. Why hadn't he tried to defend himself and the foundation if the charges weren't true? It didn't make sense.

"Did the police investigation ever discover where the stolen items came from?" she persisted, her curiosity aroused.

"They dropped the case for lack of evidence," Paul replied impatiently as if he were suddenly tired of the conversation. "Shall we get back to the rest of those files now?"

"Of course," Marnie agreed, casting one last glance at the snake goddess. Ross's past would probably remain as shadowed as the origins of this tiny sculpture, she thought to herself. No one seemed very eager to dredge up Atlantis all over again. The professor, Paul and even Ross all appeared to be satisfied to forget the matter entirely. If only their explanations didn't leave so many unanswered questions . . . She would have to resign herself to the fact that she would probably never learn the truth.

* * *

Over a long lunch, Marnie and Professor Harte discussed the day's progress. He had spent the morning talking with the senior archaeologist on the team, a retired college professor who now devoted all of his time to field research. The professor related the highlights of his conversation, then listened as Marnie described her foray into the dig's files.

Putting their heads together, they drafted a revised outline for the proposed series of articles. They had already agreed that the first would be written by both of them; Roger Bass and the professor would then share the responsibility for the second, while the professor would write the concluding article by himself. Everyone was pleased with the arrangement.

After they finished the outline, the professor left for an overnight trip to Iráklion where he was to confer with officials at the museum. Marnie headed in the direction of the dig, carrying a small sketch pad in her bag. Settling herself on a rocky knoll overlooking the site, she began the painstaking sketches. By late afternoon, she had several drawings to add to her file. Satisfied that she deserved a break, she hurried back to the hotel to change into her swimsuit.

Half an hour later she stood on the bleached white sand of the cove surveying its familiar crescent shape with as much pleasure as the first time she had seen it just days ago. The only difference now was that no sleek gray dolphin floundered helplessly on the sand and no angry male giant pursued her with murder in his eye and vengeance in his stride. The beach was as tranquil as the soothing blue ripples lapping quietly at her feet.

If anyone had told her several days ago that she would be looking forward to a swimming date with a man she had considered to be a thief, she wouldn't have believed them. The idea would have been ludicrous.

But so many things had changed in the last couple of days. Her life had been moving at a dizzying pace ever since she had met Ross. She honestly enjoyed being with him, even if it meant holding her emotions under rigid control. Instinctively, she knew that she must protect herself from the seductive danger he represented. She didn't want to be swept off her feet. She wasn't ready for that . . . yet.

"Ahoy there, mermaid." The rousing shout halted her wandering thoughts. Turning back toward the path, she watched Ross's tall figure stride across the sand toward her. Clad in a brief pair of navy swimming trunks with a towel slung carelessly around his neck, he looked like a young Greek god.

His broad shoulders were bronzed to a golden dusk and heavily rippled with muscles. A riotous mass of ebony hair curled across his chest and tapered down toward his flat waist. Marnie's gaze shifted to his face where his sardonic grin told her that she had been caught staring.

"I hope you like what you see," Ross teased, noting the blush that blossomed across her cheeks at his words. Stopping a few feet away, he let his own gaze roam over her slender form deliberately. "You're even more beautiful than I remembered," he murmured, his smoky eyes probing hers.

Marnie felt a rush of excitement sweep through her veins. His words were like a caress; a heady wine for her to swallow. She felt her heart begin to throb in her chest as her cool poise melted under the warmth of his regard. Looking for something to distract his roving eyes, she gestured toward the wicker picnic basket swinging from his hand.

"Your lunch?" she inquired, arching a delicate brow at the basket.

"No, our dinner," he replied with a grin. "I have to

leave for Athens in a couple of hours. Some business problems there require my attention for a few days." He slanted an exaggerated frown at her. "Surely you don't object to sharing the lowly fare of a humble scholar?"

"I seriously doubt that there's a humble bone in your body. But I do promise to work on my appetite right after our swim." Planting her hands on her hips, she flashed him a challenging look. "I'll race you to the tip of that cliff out there in the water."

With a glance, Ross measured the distance from the beach to the rocky mound protruding into the Mediterranean. Smiling, he nodded his approval. "You're on!"

Together they frolicked in the salty waves, luxuriating in the sheer pleasure of being alive. Later, tired but relaxed, they emerged from the water to rest on a blanket Ross pulled from the picnic basket. The setting sun cast a rosy glow on the wisps of clouds floating over their heads.

"Are you always so well equipped?" Marnie teased, smoothing the plaid fabric flat on the sand.

"Only when I plan a seduction," he countered, propping himself up on one elbow.

"I accepted your invitation to go swimming— period," she reminded him stiffly.

"I thought my intentions were perfectly clear," he remarked with feigned surprise. "I invite a beautiful woman to swim on a secluded beach where we have complete privacy and every opportunity to get to know each other better. Can you have mistaken me for a tease?"

"I'd be as likely to mistake you for a gentleman," she answered dryly.

His deep chuckle rang with good humor. "Since I can't seem to fool you, Marnie, perhaps I'd better just come right out and make my simple request."

"What request is that?" She eyed him with caution.

"Come to Athens with me. The professor won't miss you for a couple of days, and I'll lay the Parthenon at your feet." Registering her surprised expression, he smiled reassuringly. "I promise that we'll book separate rooms at the hotel, so you needn't bring along a chaperone. Please come." His dusky eyes appealed to her.

If he only knew how much she would like that, she thought, or how his nearness intoxicated her senses. But she was too level-headed to fall for hollow promises again. After one too many bitter experiences, she had vowed to follow her head in matters of the heart, and her common sense warned her to refuse Ross's offer. After all, how much did she really know about this enigmatic man? Despite his avowal of innocence in the Atlantis scandal, his past was still a mystery to her. To go away alone with him would be the height of folly.

"I can't possibly go," she told him, shaking her head with a trace of reluctance. "I only have a limited time to spend here in Crete. The article has to be finished before I leave for home."

Without replying, Ross reached out his hand to trace the sculptured line of her cheek. Marnie felt the electric current spark between them at his touch. She tried to swallow the thick lump forming in her throat as his fingers trailed down the soft curve of her neck. It was becoming harder and harder to resist this man. His slightest touch could shake her defenses to the core. She wondered fleetingly how long she could keep them from crumbling altogether.

"Are you sure I can't persuade you to come with me?" he murmured, leaning closer.

But even as Marnie shook her head, she found herself warming to the fire kindling in Ross's dusky eyes. Without protest, she allowed herself to be gathered into his embrace. His eager lips explored hers, moving slowly over her mouth with tantalizing tenderness. She felt herself begin to respond to him with a surge of yearning that startled her with its intensity. As if it were the most natural thing in the world, she arched her body against his and wrapped her arms around his neck, drawing him against her.

Ross's tongue teased her mouth as he gently lowered her to the blanket beside him. Marnie moaned softly as her ardor rose to match his, their lips fusing with the heat of their rising passions.

His hands stroked the curve of her waist as he stretched his body against hers. She felt a shiver of delight at the sensual friction of his rough warmth against her skin. Her fingers wove their way through the crisp waves of his rumpled hair, then down the slope of his neck to the satin-smooth muscles of his shoulders. She could think of nothing but the feel of his arms around her as his lips slid downward to nibble the silken hollow of her throat.

Before Marnie realized his intent, Ross had loosened the strings of her bikini top, freeing her from the confinement of the flimsy fabric. His hands moved over her bare skin, massaging her swelling breasts to hard peaks of excitement. She gasped with surprise as his tongue found a stiff crest, caressing the shell-pink flesh with featherlight kisses. Riding the dizzying tides of sensation, she ached for his touch with an intensity she had never dreamed of before.

"Ross!" She whispered his name in a voice that she hardly recognized as her own.

He raised his head to gaze down at her, tenderness shining in his dark eyes. "Now tell me that you won't come with me," he muttered thickly.

Inhaling a quick breath to steady her hammering heartbeat, Marnie stared up at him in stunned silence.

The earth seemed to reel above her head. How stupid she had been! He had intended the trip to Athens to be a cheap weekend fling. His promise of separate rooms had been a joke. It had been foolish of her to be tempted by the idea even for a second. She longed for the rocklike security of his embrace, but not on those terms. Never on those terms!

"No!" she choked out. "I won't go with you."

"I'll have to try a little more persuasion then," he responded with a provocative grin. His hands reached out to pull her closer.

"You are an arrogant, egotistical animal!" she fumed, slipping hastily out of his reach. "How dare you try and seduce me on a public beach. I wouldn't even go around the block with you after this!"

"You weren't exactly trying to fight me off a few minutes ago," Ross pointed out, lifting his brows in a lazy arch. "Now come back here and settle down. If you play your cards right, I just might forgive you for calling me those rude names."

"I can think of a few more names I'd like to call you," she countered.

"Let's not play games, Marnie," he responded with a hint of sternness in his tone. "We both know what we want."

"I don't want you to touch me," she snapped, edging off the blanket. "I'm tired of your games."

"You're the one who's playing games," he grated, watching her with narrowed eyes. "It's obvious to me that we're attracted to each other. Why do you keep trying to deny it?"

"It's obvious to me that you're accustomed to taking far too much for granted," she answered, glaring at him. Her cool poise gained a little ground as she refastened her bikini. Wishing her fingers would stop trembling, she reached for her beach robe and pulled its soft folds around her shoulders in a protective gesture.

"Do I frighten you?" Ross's voice sounded strained but less angry.

Scrambling to her feet, Marnie shook her head in wordless denial. She was careful to maintain a safe distance between them. "I just want you to leave me alone."

"It feels so right between us, Marnie." His tone softened as if he were soothing a spooked filly. "Don't you ever follow your heart, little skeptic?"

"I listen to my common sense," she replied, meeting his gaze. "It hasn't let me down yet."

"And your common sense won't allow you to come to Athens with me?"

"No," she answered firmly.

Ross's eyes shifted to study the thin black line of the horizon. Marnie could see a muscle twitch along the curve of his jaw. Expelling a deep sigh, he turned to stare back at her.

"Someday I'm going to break through that armor you wear around, and then we'll come back to this cove as lovers," he vowed. He crooked a determined smile at her startled expression. "Now let's eat. I have a plane and pilot waiting for me."

Long after Ross had left for the airport, Marnie lingered over a thick tome in the study. Restless and unsettled by their exchange in the cove, she had decided to bury herself in work. But her note pad remained blank and her pen still as concentration failed her for the first time in years. She had stared at the same pages without comprehension for hours.

If Ross only knew how close he had already come to cracking through her armor . . . She shivered. He was the only man since Rick whom she hadn't been able to keep at arm's length with ease. The only man she hadn't wanted to keep at arm's length. . . .

Unbidden, memories of Rick flooded her consciousness. Happy, carefree, reckless Rick. They had met one radiant Sunday afternoon at a tea given by one of the university's deans. The first crisp, golden days of a Chicago autumn had taken on a special aura for Marnie, warmed by the exhilarating presence of Rick by her side. It was a glow that she had mistaken for love. And when Rick had pleaded, then demanded, that she move in with him and become his "lady"—he had termed it a trial marriage—she had listened, asking him only for a little time to think things out.

Marnie had arranged to spend a long weekend by herself at her family's secluded cabin on Lake Michigan. There, after hours of strolling through the pine-scented woods and much earnest soul-searching, she had made her decision. She had left at dawn the next morning eager to hurry back to Chicago and Rick.

But the scene that greeted her at the apartment she shared with an attractive brunette nursing student had shattered her happy dreams. She had found Rick and her roommate Teresa together, their sleepy, flushed faces testimony to the sobering situation.

Teresa had moved out that afternoon, and Rick had pleaded for Marnie's forgiveness. But the damage was done. Marnie knew that she would never be able to trust Rick again.

Gradually her raw grief had turned into a chilling numbness that pervaded her every waking hour. With single-minded resolve, she had thrown herself into her studies, vowing to never let a man hurt her again. The following year she had graduated at the top of her class and received job offers from several prestigious universities. But it had been a very long time before she could face her memories of Rick again without that familiar twist of pain. It had been a cruel lesson, but one that she would never forget.

The experience had left her justifiably cautious about relationships. With a cool detachment that occasionally turned icy if a date stepped out of line, she had forced herself to attend campus functions, concerts and parties. The men who had accompanied her had all been attractive and interesting, but none of them were a match for her deliberate poise. Ross was the exception to the rule. His powerful masculinity drew her attention like a magnet and left her confused about her own emotions.

She would be taking an enormous risk if she continued to see him. The cracks in her armor of self-control had been very real this evening, she admitted grimly. Ross had made it plain that he was only interested in an affair. She would be a fool to believe that he might honestly come to care for her.

Her reverie was broken by a light knock on the door. Looking up from the book in front of her, she saw Paul standing in the doorway balancing two steaming mugs of coffee on a small tray.

"How about a break?" He flashed her his shy, owlish smile. "I saw the light and thought you might like some refreshment. Everyone else seems to have gone to bed."

Marnie glanced down at her watch in surprise. "I guess I just lost track of the time, Paul. I wasn't planning on burning the midnight oil tonight."

Stretching back in her chair, she thanked him with a smile as he placed the mug in front of her. The pungent aroma of freshly brewed coffee filled her lungs and cleared the cobwebs of memories from her mind.

"I requested some additional material from the foundation's office in Athens for you this afternoon," he said conversationally. "I asked them to send it with

Ross when he returns, so that should speed up the process by a few days."

"Your efficiency is very much appreciated," she assured him. "I hope Ross realizes what a model assistant he has."

"I take pains to remind him every year when my salary comes up for review." Paul grinned. "So far it's worked admirably."

"Good for you. When do you expect Ross to return?"

"Sometime over the weekend. Sandra is meeting him in Athens on Friday, and then they'll make plans to fly back here together. She's his uncle's stepdaughter, and a very swanky lady. Quite a morale booster for all the single men around here."

"Is she an archaeologist, too?" Marnie inquired, glancing curiously at Paul. His voice had contained a note of enthusiasm that she hadn't heard before. As her eyes met his, he turned toward the bookcase behind him and abruptly began to straighten a jumbled stack of books.

"Sandra is a model for a very elegant Parisian designer," Paul explained wistfully. "She's more at home in front of a camera than at a dusty dig site. I don't think she finds archaeology very interesting. She prefers to move in livelier circles."

"Sounds like you might just have a tiny crush on the lady," Marnie teased him gently, closing the book in front of her with a soft thud. She noticed the flush tinting Paul's normally pale complexion.

"Sandra has eyes only for Ross." He shrugged philosophically. "They make a very handsome couple."

"I see," Marnie responded, swallowing the sudden lump in her throat. A surge of conflicting emotions tightened in her chest like a vise, making it difficult to breathe. With a weary gesture, she gathered up her notebooks and rose from her chair. "I'm suddenly very tired, Paul. I guess it's time to call it a night. Thanks for the coffee."

"Anytime." He gave her an apologetic grin. "I hope the caffeine doesn't keep you awake."

"I'll be asleep by the time my head hits the pillow," she promised, heading for the door. "Good night."

But as Marnie laid in bed a short time later, her tumultuous thoughts kept sleep at bay. Twisting and turning until the sheet lay in a rumpled heap at her feet, she tried to calm her restless nerves.

Common sense told her that Ross's relationships with other women shouldn't matter to her. After all, hadn't she realized from the beginning that he was out of her league? That was a fact that his velvet charm often made her forget. And she had no claims on his attention. Why should she care if a dozen Parisian models were throwing themselves at his feet?

Unwilling to answer that question, Marnie focused her thoughts instead on their clash at the cove that afternoon. She knew that Ross had been playing a game with her, hoping to overcome her better judgment with his caresses. There was no doubt in her mind now that he was bent on luring her into an affair. He had made his intentions very clear.

She felt a sharp sting of emotion as she realized that her lack of control this afternoon had played right into his hands. Her guard had relaxed just enough to encourage his desire to crack her deliberate poise. She probably represented a rare challenge to his oversized ego, she told herself. Ross Landry wasn't accustomed to women who refused to jump right into bed with him. She had been foolish to succumb to his kisses even for a few minutes. It had only added fuel to the fire!

She would not let it happen again, she promised herself as she stared up at the ceiling. When Ross returned, he would not take up where he had left off.

She would be steeled against his magic. She would deflect his advances with deliberate indifference. He would find her armor hardened into iron.

But the stirrings of Marnie's heart were not so easily controlled. It was almost dawn before sleep overcame the gnawing, uneasy ache and the vivid memory of Ross's embrace.

Chapter Five

Marnie stared at the bulging file lying on the table in front of her. In the days since Ross's departure for Athens, she had pushed herself tirelessly, working long hours at the dig during the day and organizing her research notes in the evenings. She had compiled plenty of material to use for the first article in the series. She and Professor Harte planned to begin writing the first draft in the morning.

With luck they might finish early enough for her to spend a couple of days in Athens before she returned home. Somehow that prospect didn't seem nearly as exciting as it had when she had arrived in Crete, she acknowledged with a sigh. It was doubtful that her world would truly return to normal again until she had put the miles of the Atlantic Ocean between herself and Ross. If only the feelings he aroused could be easily distanced as well . . .

Pushing the heavy oak chair back tiredly, she decided that she deserved an early bedtime tonight. Sleep had been difficult lately, even when she had allowed herself the time. Most nights she'd stayed awake watching the shadows flicker across the wrought-iron balcony outside her room. It was only as the first pale rays of dawn streaked the sky that she found solace in dreams. Perhaps a leisurely swim in the pool would relax her tonight and let sleep come more readily.

Half an hour later Marnie stood poised on the diving board above the crystal-clear water. Except for the tinkle of glasses and the low murmur of voices from the terrace, the evening was quiet. The mirrorlike ripples of the pool below her were illuminated by the soft beams of overhead lights. A lone pine cast a deep shadow across one corner of the water.

Diving into the pool, she swam lap after lap, stretching and toning her cramped muscles. The silken fingers of the water soothed away all the tensions in her body and made her feel as nimble as a sea nymph. Relishing the tranquillity of having the pool to herself, she was glad that she had opted for a sandwich in the study while finishing up the file. Most of the other archaeologists were just settling down to dinner after cocktails at the terrace bar.

Grabbing a rubber air mattress, Marnie hoisted herself aboard and lay back in total relaxation. She lost all track of time, her thoughts drifting as aimlessly as the mattress beneath her. She thought she must be dreaming when she heard Ross's familiar baritone floating across her consciousness. Ross wasn't here, she told herself. He was miles away in Athens . . . unless he had returned early.

Opening her eyes with a start, she saw that she had drifted into the dark end of the pool. She was still alone, the poolside was deserted. Ross's voice must have come from the terrace yards away.

Paddling toward the edge of the pool, she peered through the hedge of oleanders. Thank goodness she had floated into the shadow of the pine! The rest of the pool was clearly visible from where Ross stood on the terrace.

He was talking with several members of the research team. Marnie's heart twisted painfully in her chest at the sight of his rugged profile. Her eyes traced the outline of his masculine frame clothed in a tailored pin-striped suit. He was undeniably the handsomest man she had ever seen.

Her attention shifted abruptly as a sultry brunette floated through the terrace doors and attached herself to Ross's arm. A designer gown of flaming silk molded itself to the contours of her thin figure. Long, ebony tresses were swept up into an elaborate twist, displaying the grace of her swanlike neck. The woman looked as though she had just stepped from the glossy pages of a continental fashion magazine. There was no doubt in Marnie's mind that this must be Sandra.

Paul's description of her as a "swank" lady didn't do justice to the breathtaking beauty now leaning possessively against Ross's arm. Her large, deep-set eyes, hollowed cheeks and cultured air were in the finest traditions of a haute couture model. She even looks Parisian, Marnie thought with a sigh.

As Ross turned to address another member of the group, she caught a clearer view of his face. He seemed happy and content, clearly enjoying the convivial company around him. Looking at him, Marnie felt a cold, dull ache swell in the pit of her stomach.

The cad! She slapped the surface of the water with a flash of anger, her clenched fist spraying droplets in every direction. She had been more than satisfied with her life until Ross came along. True, there were times when she had been lonely and blue, feeling a void that her career and friends just couldn't fill. But her heart had been safe and her emotions stable. She wasn't at all sure she could say that now. Why had she ever exposed herself to such a risk? Why hadn't he just left her alone!

She waited until the group on the terrace moved on to the dining room before she climbed out of the pool and slipped up to her room. She was in no mood to cross paths with Ross tonight. Better yet, she wished that she might avoid him permanently. If only the article was finished so that she could leave Crete and all its memories behind her!

After a tepid shower, she climbed into bed with the dullest book she could find, hoping to lull herself to sleep. But her careening emotions refused to be calmed. Despite the boring novel and her tiring swim, it was almost dawn before she slept. It was a pattern that was becoming increasingly difficult to break.

She awoke the next morning with a headache that lingered through her third cup of coffee. After throwing herself into writing the rough draft with more energy than she felt, she was relieved when the morning passed quickly. Seated in a quiet corner of the study, she and the professor didn't even stop for lunch. A white-coated waiter delivered salads and tea from the terrace café.

It was almost three o'clock before they declared themselves to be satisfied with the progress they had made. They agreed to spend the rest of the afternoon at the dig and then start on the article again early the following morning.

Marnie was grateful for the heavy work load. At least it helped her to keep her mind off Ross for a few hours at a time. Although she had seen no sign of him since last evening, she had resigned herself to the fact that she couldn't avoid him indefinitely. The research group was too small for her to think she might lose herself in the crowd. She only hoped that her poise and quick tongue wouldn't fail her at the critical moment.

Despite her mental preparations, it was still a shock when she saw Ross approaching that evening. Her first instinct was to run for cover, but her pride rebelled against that impulse. He was the one who was playing games. She was determined to show him that she no longer had any patience for his flirtatious advances.

Her cool glance flickered over him as he strode across the lobby toward her. He was dressed in tailored white slacks and a navy sports coat. A silk shirt stretched smoothly over his broad chest. His dark hair lay in a jumble of windblown curls as if he had just stepped from behind the wheel of his convertible. Marnie pointedly turned her gaze back to Paul as Ross neared.

"I've been looking for you since last evening, my dear. Have you been hiding yourself at the dig all this time?" His eyes roamed over her dusty clothes with undisguised warmth. "I'd hoped that you might be on hand to welcome a weary traveler home."

"I've been working long hours," Marnie replied, meeting his gaze with studied indifference. "I'm afraid I don't have time to play hostess for you or anyone else at present." The superficial sweetness of her tone belied the subtle sting of her words.

Ignoring Paul's quick glance of surprise, Marnie averted her gaze to scan the lobby around them. Out of the corner of her eye, she could see Ross studying her as if to gauge the pull of the undercurrents between them. Surely she didn't have to draw a picture for him!

"A man can always dream, can't he?" Ross replied with a sardonic arch of his brow.

"As long as he keeps his dreams to himself," she countered, ignoring his penetrating gaze. Let him draw his own conclusions from her coolness, she told herself stubbornly. He deserved no explanations from her.

"I was hoping that you might have time to join me

and a few friends for dinner tonight," he suggested in a softer tone. "The professor has told me how hard you've been working. You need a break."

"I'm hardly dressed for dinner," she pointed out, gesturing toward her grimy pants with the wide-brimmed straw hat she held in her hand. "I've just returned from the dig."

Glancing over Ross's shoulder, she saw Sandra sauntering up to join them. Dressed in a darling lilac jumpsuit, her pink-glossed lips were shaped into a sophisticated pout. She looked and moved like the exotic creature she was.

Favoring Paul with a quick hug, Sandra turned her attention to Ross. Wrapping her slender arms around his neck, she planted a lingering kiss squarely on his lips. Ross's mouth curved into a fond smile as he casually draped an arm across her shoulders.

"You're late, darling," Sandra chided him in a throaty whisper. "It's been so boring here all day without you."

"Crete is a long way from Paris, Sandra." Ross chuckled lightly. "We have to make our own excitement here."

"Well, if Paul hadn't taken pity on me and saddled up your palomino, I would have spent the entire afternoon languishing at the pool." She shrugged, smiling up at him lazily. "I've been looking forward to dinner all day. Are you ready to go?"

"I'm trying to persuade my young friend here to join us this evening," Ross responded, inclining his head toward Marnie. "Sandra, this is Marnie Chandler. Marnie, Sandra Stover, my cousin."

Marnie nodded a polite greeting, noting that the dark-haired beauty turned to really look at her for the first time. Sandra eyed Marnie's dusty jeans and smudged shirt with a fleeting glance of distaste. Her features returned to their customary pout.

"It's a pleasure to meet you, Miss Chandler," she replied, turning her gaze once again to Ross.

"Marnie is an archaeologist," Ross explained, his eyes gleaming with amusement. "She and Professor Harte are writing an article about our work here."

"How nice," Sandra murmured blandly. She flashed Ross a melting smile. "Darling, I'm positively starving."

"Please reconsider and come along with us," Ross urged Marnie, ignoring Sandra's clinging hand on his sleeve. "We'd be happy to wait for you to change."

"Not this evening. I'm rather tired," Marnie replied, turning to Paul. "I'd like to look over that information you requested for me from Athens, Paul. Would you show me where it is?"

Casting a curious glance from Marnie to his frowning boss, Paul nodded. "Sure, I have it in my office."

With a curt nod, Marnie moved away with Paul, engaging him in a spirited conversation until they were out of earshot. She felt Ross's gaze boring into her back all the way across the lobby. Surely now he would understand that she wanted him to leave her alone!

The pattern of the next two days remained much the same. Marnie spent most of the day closeted with Professor Harte, poring over their draft. On the few occasions when she ran into Ross, she made a point of treating him with indifference. When he spoke to her, she responded in an aloof manner. Each time they met she silently congratulated herself on the cold shoulder she turned toward his dogged overtures.

But her patience was wearing thin by the third evening after his return. He had waited for her outside the study that afternoon, like a hawk would its prey. Blocking her path, he had insisted that she have dinner with him. Fortunately, the professor had followed her from the room and unwittingly engaged Ross in conversation. Marnie had jumped at the opportunity to slip away from them. She could still see the angry glint in Ross's eyes as she had made her escape.

His persistence was downright annoying under the circumstances, she thought to herself. She had made her feelings clear. Surely he had gotten the message by now. So why was he being so obtuse? Ego, that was the only explanation for his stubborn behavior. Ross Landry simply wasn't accustomed to being rejected by a woman.

She reached for the pocket calendar lying on her dresser. It would take another week to wrap up the work on the article. That timetable would still allow her four days in Athens before she had to return home. Until then she would just have to keep dodging Ross's unwanted advances.

She was grateful that the professor had declared that tomorrow would be a holiday for them both. The article was shaping up nicely, and they deserved a little free time. She had accepted Paul's invitation to drive to Iráklion and spend the day at a museum. He had told her that the collection of Minoan treasures there was unequaled anywhere else in the world. It would be wonderful to get away from the hotel for a day. Her cold war with Ross was taking a taxing toll on her nerves.

Glancing at her watch, she saw that she had been reading over her notes far longer than she had intended. It was late, and they planned an early start in the morning. Closing her notebook, she rose and padded over to the open balcony door. The evening breeze caressed her skin, its gentle breath rippling her silken nightgown around her ankles. The air was laced with the sweetness of jasmine, a fragrance she would always associate with Crete—and with Ross.

A deep chuckle accompanied by the low murmur of voices drew her attention to a couple approaching the hotel on the path below her balcony. Aware that she would be silhouetted by the light from her room, Marnie stepped back and flipped off the table lamp. In the dim reflection shining from the lanterns on the terrace, she recognized Ross and Sandra. They were dressed in beach robes, obviously just returning from a late-night swim in the cove.

The thought formed an instant lump in Marnie's throat. She had first met Ross at the cove, and somehow she had come to think of it as a very special place. But that was before she had realized how vulnerable she was to his charm, and before she had called a halt to his egotistical games. Men like Ross might relish fleeting affairs with young associates like herself, but they always married exotic beauties like Sandra.

Turning away from the balcony, Marnie fled to the safety of her bed. At least in dreams she could find relief for her aching heart and an escape from the hopeless desires stirring deep within her.

As she had expected, Paul was an informative, undemanding companion. He had amused her on the drive from the hotel to Iráklion with anecdotes of his adventures in Greece during the last few years. Now he escorted her through the museum's exhibits as if he were accustomed to doing it every day of his life. Although he had seen the displays of pottery and jewelry countless times before, he listened to her exclamations of delight over each new discovery, often adding enlightening tidbits of information.

He took special care to show her the famous exhibit of sealstones with Linear B script, explaining that they had first attracted the attention of English archaeologists at the turn of the century. Crete's subsequent independence from Turkish rule gave the Englishmen the opportunity to start excavations and, ultimately, to discover the foundations of the forgotten Minoan civilization at nearby Knossos. That famous excavation site was one side trip Marnie had promised herself she wouldn't miss making before leaving Crete.

It was well past noon before they decided to stop for a light meal. They had made impressive headway through the spacious rooms on the first floor of the museum. They agreed to save the *crème de la crème* of the collection, the world renowned frescoes, until after lunch.

"I'm a familiar face around here by now," Paul told her as they seated themselves at a sidewalk café around the corner from the museum. "I eat here almost as often as the cook."

"Well, the waiter certainly treated you like a member of the family. He gave us the best table here." Marnie smiled at him across the white linen draping the table. "What do you recommend?"

"The food isn't fancy, but it *is* delicious," he replied. "Try either the calamari or the souvlaki. They're both excellent."

"I'm almost sorry that I waited so long to visit the museum," Marnie confessed after the waiter left with their order. "The collection is so interesting that I wish it had been one of my first stops in Crete. At least I managed to find the perfect guide to accompany me." She noted the pleasure that softened Paul's scholarly expression.

"I admit that I enjoy each trip to the museum almost as if it was my first. I come here several times a month on business related to the dig, and I'm afraid I'm a hopeless tourist at heart," he admitted with a smile.

They were interrupted by the waiter who served them small plates of sliced cucumbers smothered in a spicy yogurt sauce.

"Greek meals traditionally begin with some form of appetizer," Paul told her. "It may be as simple as a bit of cheese and olives or as elaborate as a small meal."

"This is delicious," Marnie declared, tasting a creamy mouthful. "I like everything I've seen of Greece, but I wish I had more time to explore the rest of the country. I feel as though I'm just seeing a little piece of it."

"Why don't you consider returning next year?" Paul suggested. "The foundation sponsors a few summer researchers each year, and I know that Ross would be delighted to have you on the team. He thinks very highly of you."

Marnie lowered her lashes to hide the surprise in her eyes, but she couldn't conceal the blush racing across her cheeks. "I'll think about it," she hedged in a tight voice. "I'm not sure what my plans will be for next summer."

Averting her gaze to study the pedestrians strolling along the sidewalk in front of them, she told herself that she would never return. It would be unbearable to even consider working closely with Ross. She would be relieved to never set eyes on his arrogant face again. He was one memory she was determined to put behind her when she left Crete.

"Your decision wouldn't have anything to do with the Atlantis scandal, would it?" Paul asked, watching her curiously. "You seemed disturbed by it the other day when we were looking at the snake goddess."

"Not really, but it has everything to do with Ross," she admitted candidly, knowing that Paul had been puzzled by the tension between the two of them lately. "We just don't seem to be able to see eye to eye."

"Now who has a crush on whom?" he teased softly, his eyes gleaming with sympathetic understanding.

"I'm afraid it's more like a cold war." She sighed. "Ross has the tendency to be rather overwhelming at times. He likes to have his own way."

"So do we all."

Marnie arched her brow inquisitively at the tinge of sadness in Paul's tone.

Catching her gaze, he smiled and shrugged his shoulders in resignation. "Sandra left for Paris in a huff this morning because Ross refuses to finance her new movie career. She swears that she's going to marry some French millionaire. I knew that she was out of my league from the beginning, but somehow that doesn't stop one from dreaming, does it?"

"No, it doesn't," she acknowledged, swallowing hard. She knew exactly how Paul felt. Still, she couldn't halt the feeling of relief from rippling through her at the news. Despite the fact that Sandra's departure would change nothing between her and Ross, she certainly wasn't sorry to see her go.

They watched in silence as the waiter returned with the main course and glasses of freshly squeezed lemonade. The rest of the meal passed quickly with each of them lost in their own thoughts. Marnie barely tasted the succulent food on the plate in front of her. She was glad when they headed back toward the museum.

Paul excused himself at the door to the exhibit, explaining that he needed to attend to some business at the curator's office. At Marnie's assurance that she could view the frescoes quite comfortably by herself, he disappeared down the stairway.

Determined to keep her mind on the frescoes, she examined the eye-catching paintings estimated to be some four thousand years old. Taken from the walls of Minoan buildings uncovered at Knossos, the scenes depicted images of people as they went about their daily lives in ancient Crete.

She stared at a scene of bullring festivities where broad-shouldered youths and laughing, dark-eyed girls somersaulted over the backs of snorting bulls, fearlessly grabbing the beasts by their horns as they lowered their heads to charge.

The frescoes were exquisite, but they might as well have been subway posters for all the attention she was paying them. Every male figure in the paintings somehow reminded her of Ross. She simply couldn't concentrate. After restlessly retracing her steps to view all the frescoes for a second time, she wandered downstairs to a small courtyard adjoining the back of the museum. She could at least enjoy the fresh air while she waited for Paul.

The dazzling sunlight reflecting off the stark white walls of the surrounding buildings hurt her eyes after the relative darkness of the museum. Lowering her lashes against the glare, she sank down on a stone bench at one end of the tiny terrace. The area was an oasis of green leaves in a desert of hot cement. Unbuttoning the neck of her shirt, Marnie wished she had brought the straw hat she usually wore around the dig. There was no shade anywhere, and the sun was blazing down on her head with merciless intensity.

Leaning back against the bench, she turned her face away from the burning rays of sunlight and let her thoughts wander. Her world had been so serene and predictable before she had met Ross. Now, in just a short time, everything had turned topsy-turvy. She had experienced more emotional peaks and valleys in the last ten days than she'd thought possible in a lifetime. At times she felt as if she were on a careening roller-coaster with no notion of where the ride might end.

Combing her fingers through her tawny locks, she wished that she was home in her Mt. Adams townhouse overlooking downtown Cincinnati. Things would have been so much simpler if she had never come to Crete—had never met Ross Landry. Fanning herself with her hand, she wished that the sun wasn't so stifling. If only there were some shade, she thought with a sigh, drifting off into an uneasy slumber.

Some time later, she was roused by the slamming of a

car door and the metallic jingle of keys. Slanting open her eyes, Marnie saw Ross's tall figure approaching her from the direction of the parking lot. He was casually dressed in a knit shirt and slacks. Dark sunglasses hid his eyes, but she realized with a start that he had seen her. It was too late to avoid him; he was headed straight for her.

Massaging her temples with her fingers, she tried to soothe away the twinges of a dull headache. She felt tired and dizzy. Narrowing her eyes against the piercing glare of the sun, she watched Ross stride toward her. Somehow she didn't quite trust herself to stand up.

"If it isn't the most elusive lady in Crete," Ross observed in a gravel tone, halting just inches from where she sat. "Are you getting tired of avoiding me, or did I catch you in a weak moment?"

"I was hoping that you'd have the sense to leave me alone," she countered stiffly. "Haven't you gotten the message by now?"

"I know that I'm thoroughly sick and tired of you playing hard to get," he answered roughly. "Don't you think it's time we stopped the games?"

"I think it's time that I was leaving," Marnie told him, rising abruptly from the bench. She was in no mood for an argument.

The wave of vertigo that swept through her limbs almost knocked her clean off her feet. She swayed uncertainly, her vision blurring. She felt Ross's strong arms reach out to steady her as her knees gave way.

"What's the matter with you?" he demanded roughly. "You look as pale as a ghost."

"I don't feel well," she admitted in a weak voice. "I just need to rest for a few minutes. The trek through the museum was more exhausting than I realized."

"I don't think the exhibits normally have such an overwhelming effect on people." He lowered her gently back to the safety of the bench. The expression in his eyes was cloaked by the dark tint of his glasses. "Have you had lunch?" he inquired in a softer tone.

"Yes." She nodded listlessly. "I was fine until I came out here. Now I have a terrific headache."

"How long have you been sitting here in the sun?"

"I don't know. I guess I fell asleep."

"You have no business being out in the sun without a hat," he pointed out, looking around the terrace with a frown. "The reflection off these buildings alone is enough to give you sunstroke. It's poison to anyone with fair coloring like yours. Still dizzy?"

"A little."

"We need to get you into the shade," he decided. "Can you stand up?"

"I'm sure that I'll be perfectly all right in a moment," she told him. "Just let me sit here."

"Don't argue. You need to rest in my office for a little while." Before Marnie realized his intention, he had scooped her up into his arms. "Now lace your fingers around my neck," he instructed firmly.

Too light-headed to protest further, she complied. It was comforting to be cradled securely against him. Resting her head against the taut muscles of his shoulder, she closed her eyes and relaxed with a sigh. A few minutes later, she was settled snugly into a leather chair in a quiet office on the first floor of the museum. It felt good to be out of the sun.

"You feel like a furnace." Ross pressed his cool fingers against the feverish skin of her forehead. "It's important that you have liquids. Don't stir a muscle, I'll be right back."

"I'll be here," she promised in a low whisper, not bothering to open her eyes.

Seconds later he was back with a cold soft drink. Marnie sipped the beverage, her parched throat welcoming the tangy citrus flavor. By the time she finished, the world was no longer reeling in front of her eyes. Slowly, she was beginning to feel more like herself.

"You look better," Ross observed, watching her from his perch on the corner of the desk.

"I feel better," she assured him. "Just a twinge of headache."

"I'm glad." His lips curved into a relieved smile as his fingers reached out to stroke her cheek. The grimness had faded from his features. Their eyes met and held for a long moment. Marnie could see herself reflected in his dark orbs. What could he be thinking?

Leaning toward her, he lowered his hands to her shoulders and tilted her face up. His gentle lips pressed a light kiss against hers. She stiffened under his fingers, dropping her gaze.

"Don't be alarmed, little mermaid," he murmured. "I think I'm beginning to learn a little patience where you are concerned. Let's reestablish our truce and have dinner together tonight."

She raised her head to study his expression. There was the hint of a plea in the depths of his smoky eyes. "I would like us to be friends, but . . ." she faltered. Friendship would certainly be an improvement over the cold war between them, but could he be content with a platonic relationship? she wondered.

As if reading the thoughts behind her searching gaze, Ross smiled reassuringly. "No pressure, I promise. We'll concentrate on being friends for a while." He chuckled unexpectedly. "I do believe that's the same thing you told me on our first date."

"It was sensible advice." Her lips curved into a small smile.

"Perhaps if I keep you near, some of your common sense will rub off on me," he teased, giving her shoulder a casual squeeze with his fingers.

"Miracles do happen," she assured him primly.

"I hope you've had your fill of the museum for the afternoon," he commented, leaning back to watch her with a soft gleam in his eyes. "I think a relaxing drive through the country is just what you need."

"I believe that I've seen everything here. Paul was a superb tour guide this morning, almost as good as you." Marnie's eyes suddenly widened. "I forgot all about Paul."

"As long as my assistant limits his competitive spirit to tours of Crete, I'll turn the other cheek. But off he goes to a dig in Siberia if he gets any other ideas about you," Ross warned, arching his brows in mock-threat.

"I don't think you have anything to worry about," she pointed out. "Paul is hopelessly infatuated with Sandra."

"Unfortunately, Sandra is more than any mere mortal man can cope with." He grinned. "I'll take care of Paul while you rest." Turning away, he reached for his phone.

Twenty minutes later, they were on their way, maneuvering the sleek Mercedes along the narrow streets of Crete's largest city. Ross insisted on giving her a brief tour of Iráklion, pointing out the famous Lion Fountain that graced the central square and a restored thirteenth-century cathedral nearby. A short distance away, Marnie caught a glimpse of the impressive ramparts and fort standing guard over the bustling waterfront of the port.

They detoured a few miles out of their way to view acres of rolling land devoted to the citrus groves that were the pride of Crete. After sampling a few juicy-sweet oranges, they headed toward a seaside café for an early dinner.

By the time Ross left her at the door of her room, Marnie's headache had disappeared and she felt almost normal. She was glad that the cold war between them had ended. And Ross had been as good as his word, pressing only one chaste kiss on her lips at the end of the evening.

As she climbed into bed a short time later, she caught herself wishing that she wasn't leaving Greece in ten days. Ross had been so charming and attentive all afternoon. If only their worlds weren't so far apart she might actually have a chance to fall in love with him. She sighed as she drifted off to sleep.

Chapter Six

Marnie gazed out of the open window of the Mercedes with lazy contentment. The foothills of the mountains whizzing by reminded her of the rugged scenery of the Southwest she had seen years ago during a family vacation to California. The gentle rise of the peaks was bleached to a dusty gold under the relentless Greek sun. Splotches of green dotted the hills where clumps of scrub struggled to gain a foothold in the baked earth. She caught an occasional glimpse of a lone shepherd herding his small flock toward better pasture in the valleys between the mountains.

Stretching back against the plush contour of the passenger seat, she glanced over at Ross. His profile looked carefree and relaxed as he guided the automobile along the winding road to Knossos. The sultry breeze ruffled his hair against his forehead in dark waves. Blue-tinted sunglasses shielded his eyes from the glaring afternoon sun.

He looks dashing and handsome, she thought, her heart doing a silly flip-flop against her ribs. He was a man that any woman would be proud to have at her side.

As if sensing her eyes upon him, Ross turned his head to glance at her. A knowing smile curved his lips. They exchanged a warm look of companionship that needed no words of explanation.

The last few days had been idyllic. Ever since the renewal of their truce that afternoon at the museum, the time they spent together had been a richly woven tapestry of contentment. Marnie felt that they were well on their way to becoming real friends. The physical attraction was still present between them, but Ross had been as good as his word. He had made no demands on her. Common sense told her that this was exactly what she had wanted.

Only one cloud shadowed their newfound pleasure in each other's company. Marnie felt her days on Crete slipping away too swiftly. No matter how sternly she cautioned herself against it, the dream that someday Ross might learn to care for her still haunted her. Despite the fact that he had given her no indication that he desired anything more than a brief summer fling, the hopeless longings remained in her heart.

She was planning to leave Crete on schedule next week, but she had promised herself the satisfaction of enjoying his company until then. At least she would have the bittersweet memories to warm her lonely nights at home. It was impossible to ask for more than that.

Ross slowed the car to maneuver around a yellow tour bus that had stopped to unload passengers near the entrance to the excavations. Continuing on, he took a sharp right turn. The tires crunched noisily against the gravel drive as he pulled into a private parking lot adjoining the small museum.

"Rank has its privileges." He grinned as they climbed out of the Mercedes.

"Just like beauty and old age," she observed sweetly.

"Something like that. Now if you'll get the picnic basket out of the trunk while I let Professor Demetrious know we're here, we can be on our way."

At her nod, he tossed her the car keys and headed toward the museum door. Marnie smoothed the wrinkles from her blue-and-white-striped seersucker skirt and walked around to the back of the car. The trunk glided open as she turned the key. Stashing Ross's initialed key ring in her pocket, she pulled the basket out onto the bumper. The sleeve of a green nylon jacket Ross had left in the trunk caught on the wicker handle.

Balancing the basket with her hips, she reached across to yank the jacket loose. As it came free, she heard a dull thud echo against the floor of the trunk. Peering inside, she glimpsed the bright flash of metal.

Setting the picnic hamper on the ground, she reached for the exquisite gold medallion that had fallen out of the pocket of Ross's jacket. Its delicate sunburst shape fit easily into the palm of her hand. She held it up toward the light to admire the handcrafted skill that had fashioned the unique design.

Sunlight glittered off the detailed figure of Apollo as he drove his mighty chariot on his daily journey across the heavens. His whip cracked above the heads of his galloping steeds with lifelike spirit. The ebbing features of the goddess of the moon could be seen in the filigree background as daylight symbolically supplanted the darkness of the night.

Marnie didn't need to be told that the medallion was of museum quality. The ancient craftsman who had perfected it had used solid gold, judging from its weight. She wondered why Ross had stuck such a rare piece so carelessly in the trunk of the Mercedes. Any museum would have been proud to place it on exhibit.

She heard voices and turned to see Ross emerging from the brick building with a bearded companion in tow. Stuffing the medallion back into his pocket, she stowed the jacket in the trunk and slammed it closed. She would ask him about it later.

"So this is the young lady you have been telling me about." Professor Demetrious eyed her with open admiration. "Why didn't you tell me that you had such a beautiful researcher hidden away at your dig? I would have been happy to sacrifice hours of my time just to satisfy her thirst for knowledge!"

Ross flashed her a conspiratorial wink. She had been warned by Sarah Harte that most Greek men were inveterate flirts when it came to foreign women. Here, she was sure, was a prime example of such behavior.

Bowing as he reached for her hand, the swarthily attractive young professor raised it to his lips in gallant tribute. His piercing eyes regarded her with unabashed delight.

"I am afraid, beautiful lady, that if I were one of your students, I should learn nothing of archaeology in your class."

"If you applied yourself, I'm sure you'd be my star pupil," she assured him with an amused smile.

"Impossible!" he declared. "I would spend all my time composing sonnets to your beauty."

"Don't lay it on too thick, Spiro," Ross warned. "She might decide that she prefers Greek men over American."

"In that case, my friend, I will gladly take her off your hands. I would marry her in an instant!"

"Over my dead body," Ross growled in exaggerated menace. "Not even Zeus could save you from my wrath."

Shaking hands with Ross in good-natured camaraderie, Spiro waved them on their way. "I apologize that I cannot give you a personal tour this afternoon, but we have officials arriving from Athens. Please return when we can visit longer." He bowed in Marnie's direction.

"Greek men are definitely charming," Marnie commented dryly as they strolled along the path leading to the excavations. The oleanders lining the walkway were in full bloom, displaying their fragile petals in splashes of red, white and pink profusion. They detoured around a cluster of German students who were receiving a lecture from their tour leader. The youths' fresh, shining faces were intent.

"Don't let Spiro's aura of local color deceive you," Ross warned. "He was educated in the United States. I first met him when we were both graduate students."

"No wonder he speaks such perfect English," she exclaimed.

"His wife probably has something to do with that. I believe she's from Vermont. An American wife is considered a status symbol among Greek men, you know." Ross slanted her an amused glance.

"Marriage certainly hasn't put a damper on his propensity to flirt," she observed.

"Some men just aren't the marrying kind." Ross shrugged carelessly.

Marnie glanced up at him sharply. Had he meant those words for her? she wondered. Turning away in confusion, she let her eyes roam over the hills surrounding the ancient city. Clumps of tall cypress and silver-leafed olive trees flourished on the otherwise barren knolls. The endless blue of the sky stretched in unblemished splendor over the peaks of the distant mountains. It was beautiful, but somehow empty . . . like the hollow ache within her.

She was reminded once more that she would probably never see Ross again after she left Crete. The bustling, wheeling-dealing world of Wall Street was far removed from that of a tree-lined college campus. Ivory towers and financial empires just didn't belong together. They lived in two different worlds, even if Ross did manage to escape his for a few weeks every year. His place was in the ranks of high-powered financiers with their gambling instincts and jet-set mores. Marnie knew in her heart that she could never be a part of that life-style.

Although she had fought against her attraction to Ross from the very beginning, she had to admit that she was glad they were now friends. Unconsciously, he had forced her to face a part of herself that she thought had died after Rick's betrayal. Because of Ross, she was learning to trust her feelings again, to let her emotions have sway over her hard-boiled common sense. It was a difficult lesson, but one she hoped would enrich her life after they went their separate ways—after she was gone.

"Have I lost you already, little mermaid?" Ross's mellow baritone broke through her reverie.

Marnie glanced up at him in surprise. Did he feel something, too?

But the lazy grin softening his bronzed features wiped that thought from her mind. He was teasing her, referring to his role of tour guide.

"I'm waiting for the lecture to start," she told him airily. "Every tour worth its salt begins with an explanation of the significance of what we are about to see."

"I wouldn't dream of disappointing a lady." His eyes gleamed with a warm light as he launched into his introductory remarks. "The ruins of Knossos were reconstructed by a group of English archaeologists around the turn of the century. Their discovery of an elaborately structured palace at this site confirmed what some historians had always suspected: a sophisticated civilization existed on Crete around 1600 B.C. At that time most of Europe was little more than groups of barbaric tribes."

"That would make Crete one of the oldest civilizations in the history of the world," Marnie mused.

"Correct." He nodded. "The island was ruled by a succession of priest-kings dedicated to a strange religion over which bulls held a strong influence. You'll see bull motifs everywhere in the reconstructed palace."

"But no present-day Minotaurs, I hope." She smiled.

"I'm afraid not. The golden days of the Minoan empire and the Minotaur came to an end around 1450 B.C., destroyed by invasion, volcanos or tidal waves. No one knows for sure. After that the island degenerated into primitive city-states, much like the rest of the world at that time."

"Leaving the remnants of a broken civilization behind," Marnie reflected.

"Just waiting for eager archaeologists like us. Let's start here and work our way around the courtyard. We'll save the throne room for last."

Two hours later, Marnie felt as though she had been given the royal tour of Knossos. Ross had painstakingly explained every detail concerning the palace and the lives of its ancient inhabitants, laying the wonders of the Minoan empire at her feet.

"I doubt that Professor Demetrious himself could have put together a more enlightening tour," she teased him as they paused to rest. From where they sat on the sloping hillside, the ruins looked like a maze of crumbling walls and foundations. Only the reconstruction efforts of dedicated archaeologists had saved the palace itself from disintegrating into rubble.

"Spiro would be interested in expanding more than just your horizons," he responded dryly. "Beware of the flattery of Greek men."

"It's not Greek men that I'm concerned about," she

replied. "Their intentions are so transparent that it's almost amusing to watch them in action."

"I hope you don't have any doubts about my intentions, my dear." Wrapping a muscular arm around her shoulders, he pulled her against him. "Your fate has already been decided. You may fight against it now, but someday it will be my turn to call the shots," he murmured against her ear.

His warm breath sent a quiver of sensation prickling along her nerves. "I'll be safely back in Cincinnati in a few days, and then you'll forget all about me," she countered.

"Haven't you learned by now that it's dangerous to make such sweeping assumptions, little mermaid?" His dusky eyes mocked her gently. "But let's not quibble. I have something for you." Reaching into the pocket of his sports shirt, he drew out a small jeweler's box. "Open it," he said, placing the box in the palm of her hand.

Marnie lifted the black satin lid to disclose a sculptured gold dolphin suspended from a delicately woven chain. The details etched into the burnished metal made the creature look breathtakingly real. Its eyes sparkled with the glittering fire of two brilliant diamonds.

"It's beautiful," she whispered in rapt admiration.

"It's for a beautiful woman," Ross responded, fastening the pendant around her neck. "A keepsake to remember the rescue of our dolphin." His fingers lingered against her throat, caressing the slender curve of her neck.

Marnie felt her blood kindle at the sensual patterns his fingertips traced along her skin. He inclined his head to press a gentle kiss on her expectant lips, moving his mouth in a slow, tantalizing rhythm. Her hand slid up to cradle the back of his head, her fingers losing themselves in his crisp dark hair. She felt her heart throbbing against the wall of his chest as her feminine curves molded against him like soft wax.

This was the first time in days that he had really kissed her. The dormant longing for his touch welled inside of her with exquisite sweetness. She pulled him closer, yearning for more. She wanted to lose herself in the ambrosial taste, feel and smell of him.

He raised his head to stare down into her flushed face. His smoky eyes probed hers for what seemed an eternity. "This is neither the time nor the place," he muttered huskily. "I think you'd better feed me now, woman, or I won't be responsible for the consequences."

In an attempt to control her racing emotions, Marnie lurched to her feet. Deep breathing calmed her pounding heart as she busied herself with straightening her blouse, tucking the loose folds into the waistband of her skirt. She glanced at Ross, who sat staring out at the panoramic view that surrounded them. It was impossible to decipher his expression.

Her common sense told her that he was wise to have stopped their lovemaking before it went too far. There was no point in spoiling their friendship with vain longings and hopeless desire. Their relationship would end soon enough. But her heart couldn't dismiss the sharp sting of disappointment so easily. It had felt so right to be in his arms.

She pulled a red-and-white gingham cloth from the hamper and began to spread out their meal. They dined on the cold roast chicken, cheese and fruit with undisguised relish. The small bottle of retsina contributed a mellow spirit to the waning afternoon. The fiery orb of the sun had sunk behind the ridge of the mountains by the time they stowed the empty basket in the trunk and started back to the hotel.

The hum of the Mercedes engine soon lulled Marnie to sleep. She awoke as Ross turned the car into the hotel parking lot and switched off the ignition. With a start, she realized that she was snuggled up against him, cushioning her head on his shoulder. She had no idea how long she had slept in that position.

"Wake up, sleeping beauty. We're here." He gave her a gentle shake.

"I'm awake." She sat up, muffling a yawn with the back of her hand. "I'm sorry I fell asleep, but you can't ply me with wine and then expect me to entertain you with scintillating conversation."

"I'll have to remember that." Ross smiled through the darkening twilight. "Now what would you say to a swim in the cove before bed?"

"It sounds lovely," Marnie agreed. It would be wonderful to stretch her muscles after sitting in a cramped car for so long.

"Okay, meet me in the lobby in fifteen minutes."

"I'll be there," she promised, her sleepiness vanishing.

Humming a cheerful tune, she climbed the stairs to her room. A few minutes later, she was dressed in her apricot bikini and low-heeled sandals. She paused in front of the mirror to pull her hair back from her face and twist it into a loose braid. The emerald eyes that stared back at her from the mirror sparkled with excitement. She hadn't been for a swim in the cove for days. Her fingers wistfully fondled the gold dolphin hanging about her neck. She would cherish it for the rest of her life.

Pulling her chenille beach robe around her shoulders, she tied it at the waist with the fringed sash. She packed a towel in her canvas carryall and headed for the door. Tonight she would relax and enjoy herself. After all, she had promised herself a healthy store of memories of their time together. The parting would come far too soon.

Ross was waiting for her in the lobby, balancing a vinyl cooler in the crook of one arm and a towel and flashlight in the other.

"Ready?"

"All set," she confirmed with a brisk nod.

The path through the deserted olive grove echoed with the soft patter of their footsteps. Ross swung the beam of the flashlight out in front of them like a lighthouse beacon. The darkness was punctuated by the chirping of crickets. A bright sliver of moon lit the sky.

"Let's leave the towels under this pine and wade out to those rocks with the wine," he suggested.

"Wine and moonlight?" Marnie's tone belied her pleasure.

"You can't blame a guy for trying." He shrugged. "Are you game?" He flung her a challenging look.

"Of course," she answered, covering her momentary hesitation. Just what did he have in mind? she wondered.

The water was up to her waist by the time they reached the cluster of large, flat-topped rocks. Their smooth wet surface was worn slick by the endless rush of the tides. Grasping her by the waist, Ross boosted Marnie up to perch perilously on the slippery stone, joining her himself a moment later.

He opened the zippered pouch of the cooler, pulling out two glasses and an uncorked bottle of Chardonnay. After filling the glasses, he stashed the bottle safely between his knees.

"To wine, and moonlight, and us," he toasted, touching her glass with his.

They sipped the cool, crisp wine in silence, watching the moon climb in the sky and listening to the symphony of the waves. Marnie felt the warm glow of contentment seeping throughout her limbs. Her feet dangled lazily in the swirling surf.

"One more glass of wine and then we'll go swimming," Ross proposed. He refilled her glass without waiting for her response.

Marnie slanted him a glance. The silvery moonlight silhouetted his profile, emphasizing the chiseled quality of his strong features. The light breeze ruffled the hair on his sinewy forearms and chest. She watched the muscles ripple across his shoulders as he raised his glass to his mouth. Her heart twisted with the longing to touch his hard, lean flesh.

His hand reached out to tuck a stray wisp of hair behind her ear and lingered to caress the side of her face. She unconsciously leaned toward him, forgetting her precarious balance on the wet rock. As if in slow motion, she felt herself begin to slide across the slick surface, plunging downward into the waves. His hand grazed her shoulder as he tried to stop her fall, and suddenly he was slipping too.

They surfaced together, coughing and laughing as they wiped the stinging saltwater from their faces. A little giddy from the wine, Marnie swayed uncertainly as her feet tried to find firm footing in the sand. Ross reached out to steady her. His hands moved over her as if to assure himself that she was unharmed, then he drew her against him.

Their bodies melted together as he pressed her soft curves against his hard strength. His hands massaged the small of her back, moving through the water like rippled satin. The electric current that pulsed between them kindled a fever of yearning inside Marnie.

Giving herself up to the moment, she arched her body against his. Standing on tiptoe, her arms twined around his neck as a warm hand slid around her rib cage to cup a full breast. A low moan of pleasure slipped from her throat. Her fingers trailed across the slope of his shoulder to the rocklike breadth of his chest where they traced the rough swirls of hair.

"I've tried to keep my distance, little mermaid. I don't want to scare you away," he murmured huskily.

"I . . . I'm not afraid," she whispered brokenly. Suddenly it didn't seem to matter that he didn't love her. She just wanted to feel his arms around her, to savor the sweetness of his kiss.

He lowered his head to press kisses across her brow and eyelids, working his way along the line of her jaw to her mouth. Fiery lips found hers, caressing her softness until every nerve in her body tingled with longing. His eager tongue met the moist silkiness of hers, scorching her blood like wildfire.

His mouth traveled down the curve of her neck to the hollow of her throat while restless hands stroked her feverish skin, sending ripples of sensation along her nerves. He loosened the top of her bikini, freeing the creamy mounds beneath. His lips trailed across her bare flesh, branding her nipples.

Marnie felt her breasts swell under his assault as a wave of smoldering need rose within her. She threaded her fingers through his dark hair, reveling in the wonder of his touch.

"This isn't enough, Marnie," he muttered against the cool smoothness of her skin. "A fire this strong can't be quenched. . . ."

"Ross . . ." Her sigh echoed against the night breeze. The stars above her seemed to reel across the heavens.

"We can't go on like this, little mermaid." His voice was thick with emotion. "I want you now."

"Yes! Oh, yes . . ." she whispered. She felt drunk with desire, intoxicated by a passionate yearning that only he could satisfy. The stirring ache in her heart would not be denied. If she couldn't have his love, at least she would cherish whatever part of himself he chose to give her.

She heard a gasp of surprise from Ross as his hands were suddenly torn away from her waist. She caught only a glimpse of streaking phosphorescent light before a dark, heavy weight knocked her off her feet. The salty waves closed over her head as she struggled to regain her balance. She came up choking and sputtering with the mouthful of water she had swallowed. The unexpected dive had brought her to earth with a bone-rattling thud.

"Look!" Ross's arm curved protectively around her waist as he gestured with his other hand to a darting group of shadows trailing glistening green sparks in their wake. "Dolphins!"

As they stood side by side watching the intricate water ballet, one shape again broke away from the cluster and sped in their direction. Moonlight illuminated the sleek figure skimming through the surf toward them. It swam a small circle around them before returning to its companions.

"They're inviting us to swim with them," Marnie marveled, her eyes scanning the waves in delight at the dolphins' playful antics.

"I don't appreciate their timing," Ross pointed out with a mock scowl. "But I guess we should give it a try."

Ross and Marnie were only a few feet away from their watery games before they darted away. Splashing and cavorting in joyful abandon, the dolphins reminded Marnie of a group of children let out of school for recess. Their boundless energy soon surpassed that of the two humans who waded wearily toward shore.

"They're leaving!" Marnie motioned toward the fading streaks of blue speeding from the shelter of the cove. "Weren't they wonderful?"

"Any other evening I'd probably agree with you,"

Ross commented dryly. "But there are some things, my little seductress, that just shouldn't be interrupted." Reaching for her, he laced his arms around her waist, pinning her body against his.

"Seductress!" Marnie choked, the harshness of the word piercing the evening's enchantment. She felt a ripple of shock wash over her senses. What had happened to her earlier? Had she completely thrown herself into his power? She shuddered, trying to edge away from the strange light gleaming in his dusky eyes. "Ross, I'm cold."

"Then let me warm you," he murmured against her temple, tightening his hold on her.

"No! I want to go back to the hotel," she cried, her teeth starting to chatter in earnest. She felt chilled and miserable.

"You really are cold." He frowned, suddenly staring down into her face. "You're shivering."

"I'm freezing." She dropped her eyes, not wanting him to see the confusion in their depths. The breeze off the water was cool, but she knew that it had nothing to do with the nervous quiver suddenly racking her body.

"We need to get you dried off before you catch pneumonia." A stern mask dropped over Ross's features as he marched her across the sand to the pine tree where they had stowed their towels and robes. Marnie caught her breath at the banked fires of desire that flickered in his gaze as he helped her into her robe.

It had been easy to convince herself that her defenses were still strong as long as Ross had maintained a certain amount of distance between them. But she knew in her heart that her carefully assembled pose of friendship had been no match for the passions lying dormant within them. If the dolphins hadn't appeared, there was no telling where their lovemaking might have ended.

The combination of wine, moonlight and her own

emotions had finally overwhelmed the restraints of common sense. Still trembling, she huddled deeper into the protective folds of her robe as she followed him along the winding path.

Tonight she had almost surrendered to the velvet magic of a man bent upon luring her into the shortest of summer flings. A man who had unequivocally fulfilled his promise of breaking through her armor of self-control. If the dolphins hadn't appeared, Ross would know by now that she was hopelessly in love with him. It had been a very close call indeed. . . .

Chapter Seven

"Good morning, Miss Chandler. You're looking very pretty this morning." Georgios's dark-eyed gaze admired her trim figure from his vantage point behind the front desk of the hotel. His roving glance took in the shapely lines of her white slacks and the feminine drape of her blue silk blouse before returning to her face with a friendly smile.

An aquiline nose, raven hair and slightly cleft chin combined to give the young desk clerk an Adonis-like appearance. Marnie suspected that he had already broken a few hearts among the village girls despite his tender years; nevertheless his obvious admiration gave a pleasant lift to her morning routine. Her lips curved into a small smile.

"Flattery will get you nowhere with me, Georgios, but thank you anyway. How are the English lessons coming along?"

"Professor Harte says I am doing well. He is—how do you say—a patient man."

"He is indeed, but your progress is still astounding. Your pronunciation and vocabulary are improving every day." Her voice rang with encouragement.

"Thank you, pretty lady." He reached behind the desk for her copy of an English newspaper and handed it across the counter to her. "The professor left word that he would be on the terrace if you wish to join him."

"I'm headed in that direction right now. Thank you, Georgios."

Marnie scanned the headlines as she walked along. The newspaper was a day late by the time it reached Crete, but at least it kept her in touch with the rest of the world. A special feature about an archaeological museum in Athens caught her eye. She made a mental note to be sure to read the article later in the day when she had more time.

Stashing the paper in her shoulder bag, she paused at the entrance to the terrace. The professor was seated at a corner table, shaded by the overhanging branches of a pink bougainvillea. Only a few of the other tables were occupied. She strode across the flagstones to join him.

"Good morning, Professor. Have you ordered yet?" She dropped her bag into the empty chair between them and sat down.

Raising his snowy head, the professor looked up from the letter he was reading. "Good morning, my dear. I've ordered a pot of coffee, but I think the chef might be persuaded to rustle up something more substantial for you." He eyed her fondly over the top of his glasses. "I don't want Sarah thinking we didn't feed you."

"I'll never tell," she assured him with a mischievous twinkle in her eyes. "Coffee sounds fine. I'm really not hungry. Is that by any chance a letter from Sarah?"

"Oh yes! And brand-new pictures of the baby." He

handed two snapshots across the table. "These just arrived this morning."

Marnie examined the first photo, smiling at the small, pink face of the sleeping infant. In the second picture, the baby was staring wide-eyed into the camera, her tiny fist poised in midair.

"She has your eyes, Professor. But where did the red hair come from?" She glanced up at his beaming face. He looked as though he might burst with pride.

"Her mother had red hair when she was born," he explained. "Later it lightened to golden blond, like mine before it matured." He chuckled, gesturing to his own snowy head.

"She's beautiful. You have every right to be proud of her."

"Perhaps someday she'll grow up to be another beautiful lady archaeologist." The velvety baritone voice came from behind Marnie's chair. A shiver of apprehension tingled down her spine at the familiar sound.

She felt Ross's hands rest lightly against her shoulders as he leaned over her to peruse the snapshots. Slanting a glance at his freshly shaven profile, she breathed in a whiff of his tangy masculine scent. He was so close that his lips almost brushed her hair.

Sensing her gaze, he turned his head to smile down at her with an expression that kindled a sparkling glow in her veins. The warmth of his fingers burned her skin through the soft folds of her blouse. He looked cheerful and relaxed. His face held no hint of the troubling emotions that had kept Marnie awake until dawn.

"Why don't you join us, Ross? Perhaps you can persuade Marnie to eat something." The professor was watching them with a bemused smile on his lips.

She dropped her eyes to focus her attention on the

waiter who had appeared to fill her cup with coffee. Ross's nearness was once again unraveling her careful poise. The previous night on the way back from the cove she had promised herself that she would keep a tight rein on her emotions, but at the moment his touch was shattering her determination.

"Thank you, Professor." Ross lowered his frame into the chair next to Marnie's. "Waiter, please bring fruit and croissants for the lady." Halting her protest with a wave of his hand, he flashed her an irresistible smile. "Humor me, little mermaid. I haven't time to argue this morning. We've got a bank merger in the works that requires my immediate attention. I have to be in Athens by noon." His eyes lingered wistfully on the moist fullness of her lips. "I wouldn't go if it wasn't absolutely necessary."

"I hope your business won't take you away from us for too long," the professor commented.

His words echoed Marnie's silent thoughts. She couldn't help glancing at Ross with a hint of dismay in her green eyes. Every moment with him was becoming increasingly more precious, and she would be leaving in a few days. Although her common sense told her that she should be relieved by the news, she wasn't. She felt anxious and blue.

"I hope to have everything ironed out in a day or two," Ross explained. "I should be back by Wednesday at the latest. Marnie and I have some unfinished business of our own to settle by then." His eyes probed her face over the rim of his coffee cup.

"I think we've managed to cover all the nearby excavations and temples, haven't we?" She tried to keep her tone light, but her heart was hammering against her ribs. She wished he wasn't looking at her quite so intently. Obviously he regarded her behavior the night before as encouragement for his advances.

"That's not exactly what I had in mind. I was hoping

that I might convince you to stay in Crete . . . indefinitely."

Marnie stared at him in surprise, trying to swallow the lump in her throat. The warmth in Ross's eyes was causing her heart to flip-flop in her chest. What on earth could he mean? Had he somehow come to care for her, just a little? She dropped her eyes, reluctant to let him see the hope shining in their depths. She didn't trust herself to speak.

"I won't let you spirit away the most promising young instructor in my department, Ross Landry," the professor warned in a mock-serious tone. "Marnie is scheduled to teach a seminar this summer at the university."

"I'm sure that Professor Browne could find someone else to help him with that seminar," Ross replied. "Atlantis will be far more exciting."

"Atlantis?" Marnie echoed, frowning. An unexpected sting of disappointment lashed across her senses. Did Ross want her to stay for professional rather than personal reasons?

"I'm planning on reestablishing a research team on our old Atlantis site this fall," Ross told her. "I'm convinced that we were on the right track with that project several years ago, but once the scandal broke it was impossible to continue serious research. I was hoping that you might agree to take a leave of absence from the university and help me organize everything this summer." His eyes were lit by a strange eagerness as he watched her from across the table.

"But there are hundreds of other archaeologists who would be more qualified than me to help you," she hedged, stalling for time.

"You're the only one who will do," Ross assured her with a smile that sent a glow of happiness surging through her veins. This was the first time he had mentioned any kind of a future for them. Suddenly she wanted very much to stay.

"Let me think it over," she told him. "I'll give you an answer when you return from Athens."

"I guess I'll have to be satisfied with that for the present," he responded, a glance at his watch launching him to his feet. "I've got to get moving. Until Wednesday, little mermaid." He brushed a whisper-soft kiss across her lips.

"I'll keep her busy so she won't miss you," the professor teased.

"Thanks. I need more friends like you, Professor." With a wave of farewell, Ross turned toward the lobby where Paul stood waiting.

Marnie watched him depart with an indefinable sadness tugging at her senses. It would seem like an eternity before he returned.

"I guess that Professor Browne will be teaching the seminar alone after all." The professor's comment pulled her attention away from Ross.

"Nothing has been settled," she murmured cautiously. "I haven't decided to stay yet."

"I'd wager that it's been decided for you. You know, I don't think I've ever seen Ross in love before." His voice held a note of amused pleasure.

"I'm afraid you're mistaken," she demurred, trying to hide the shock in her eyes. Still, it was impossible to stem the heady elation racing through her blood. What if the professor was correct? Could Ross be in love with her?

"That was certainly some truce the two of you worked out," he commented dryly. "The United Nations could use people like you."

"I cultivated Ross's friendship at your request," she pointed out innocently. "He is, after all, one of the department's most important benefactors. We owe him a great deal." She repeated the very phrases he had used on her first night on Crete.

"Little did I dream that those words of wisdom would return to haunt me." His eyes sparkled with good humor. "Now eat some breakfast so we can get to work. We don't want to disappoint our worthy benefactor."

"Perish the thought," she responded, biting into a slice of ripe peach.

Hampered by her obvious lack of concentration, Marnie nevertheless managed to get through the rest of the day. She and the professor had done their work well; by the end of the afternoon all that remained was tying up a few loose ends and deciding on the illustrations that would accompany the text.

"Why don't we plan on spending time tomorrow morning at the dig," she suggested as they finished proofreading the article. "We can discuss exactly what pictures we need, and then we can give Roger a list of the subjects we want to include when he arrives with his cameras."

"That's fine with me," the professor agreed. "Let's call it a day. We should be able to wrap everything up tomorrow."

"Great! I was hoping you'd say that, Professor." She pushed her chair back from the table and sprang to her feet. Stuffing her notebooks into her bag, she swung the strap over her shoulder and headed for the study door. "I'm going for a swim!"

Rounding the corner of the hallway with her head floating among the clouds, she almost collided with Paul. He automatically reached out to grab her shoulders in an attempt to avoid knocking her off her feet.

"Terrific day, isn't it, Paul?" She beamed up at his startled face. Her green eyes danced with high spirits.

"Yes, terrific," he echoed in surprise. Suddenly his face split into a grin as he noticed her infectious cheerfulness. "It's wonderful to see you so happy, Marnie!" He gave her arms a quick squeeze before releasing her.

"Thank you, kind sir." She performed a mock curtsy before turning to hurry on her way. Was the sun really shining brighter today? she wondered as she tripped up the stairs to her room. Were the birds singing louder? Or was it just her imagination?

It didn't matter, she told herself as she slipped out of her pants and blouse. Only she and Ross and the stirrings of their hearts really mattered. She pulled the narrow straps of a one-piece burgundy swimsuit up over her shoulders. Not even a cloudburst could dampen the glow of supreme happiness she had felt since that morning. She wanted to embrace the world, to share a little of the joy radiating from her.

Leaning toward the gilt mirror, she gathered her hair off her neck and twisted it into a French braid. Her eyes stared back at her from the mirror like two emerald stars. She had realized last night that she was in love with Ross. Could it possibly be true that he loved her in return?

She gently touched the golden charm hanging at her throat. So much had happened since the day she had found the beached dolphin in the cove. Could Ross really care as much about her as she did about him? Only time would tell. She sighed. For now, she could hope . . . and dream.

Gathering her sunglasses and towel, she headed down the stairs to the pool. A leisurely swim would relax her vibrating nerves. The poolside was empty except for two little girls dangling their feet in the water at the shallow end.

Marnie dumped her possessions into a white lounge chair and strolled toward the side of the pool. Testing the temperature of the water with one tentative foot, she smiled in satisfaction. It was perfect. Without further hesitation, she dove gracefully into the cool, blue depths.

She surfaced moments later, flinging droplets of moisture out of her hair with a pert shake of her head. The rays of the sun sparkled like diamonds across the rippling surface of the water. Inhaling deeply, she began a slow crawl stroke along the length of the pool. She concentrated on the rhythm of her body, banishing all other thoughts from her mind. By the time she climbed from the pool thirty minutes later, she felt tired but tranquil.

She patted her face and shoulders dry with the towel. The warm breeze ruffled its lazy fingers through her damp locks. Her skin soaked up the sultry glow of the waning sun like a thirsty sponge. She looked around her with a glow of contentment.

The two girls were in the pool now, along with a couple of older boys. They were all splashing and cavorting noisily to their hearts' delight. Marnie knew that several of the researchers had brought their families with them for the summer, but she hadn't spared the time to connect all the names with faces. She had been too busy with her work on the article, and too preoccupied with Ross. Perhaps she would get to know the other researchers and their families better at a future date. Anything seemed possible today.

She stretched out on the white webbing of the lounger with a sigh. Plucking the morning newspaper from her bag, she adjusted her sunglasses on her nose and leaned back to scan the headlines. Things seemed very much the same. The never-ending reports of conflict and crisis were bannered across the front page in bold, heavy print. Only the names and faces changed from day to day, she reflected.

Impatient with the world's foibles on such a wonderful day, she turned to the feature concerning Athens's famous museum. This, at least, would hold her interest.

The reporter began the story with a general description highlighting the importance of the museum. He cited various exhibits that covered every period of ancient Greek civilization, ranging from simple clay relics to priceless gold treasures. He then launched into a discussion of the recent rash of museum thefts and the growing problem of the black-market trade in stolen antiquities.

The article was well-written and researched. Marnie read with interest a side-bar story about artifacts reported stolen during a recent museum break-in. But her eyes widened with disbelief as she glanced at the accompanying photos. One of them pictured a medallion that bore a startling resemblance to the one she had seen in Ross's trunk the day before in Knossos. It couldn't be the same medallion!

Her eyes moved to the short description printed under the photo. She swallowed hard. The details fit the medallion she had held in her hand. According to the article, it was definitely solid gold and valued at a fabulous sum of money. Her gaze narrowed as she stared at the picture with intense concentration. The reproduced snapshot was slightly fuzzy, but her memory wasn't mistaken. It looked exactly like the piece she had seen only yesterday.

Her attention raced back to the text of the article. The artifact had been stolen within the past few weeks, and authorities speculated that it was still in the country. Several other gold relics had been taken at the same time, but the medallion was by far the most prized of the group. A museum official was quoted as saying that the thieves would probably have little trouble selling the medal to a wealthy private collector. He urged anyone with information about the stolen goods to contact either the museum or the police.

Marnie stared at the paper in front of her until the print began to blur before her eyes. Her hands were trembling so hard she could barely hold the newspaper upright. Dropping it into her lap in disarray, she raised her fingers to her temples. Rubbing her fingertips in small, concentric circles, she tried to lessen the pain of a splitting headache.

It can't be true, she told herself over and over again. Ross couldn't be involved with thieves. There had to be some explanation, some logical reason. . . .

During their first evening together, he had demanded that she not convict him without evidence. She had made the mistake of assuming his guilt in the Atlantis scandal, believing everything she had read in the magazines and newspapers. And he had been justifiably angry with her when she had accused him of wrongdoing. But this time the situation was different. She had found a stolen artifact hidden in the trunk of his car. This time there was concrete proof.

Despite her initial misgivings, she had accepted Ross's avowal of innocence as the truth. He had seemed so sincere at the time, and the professor had been so quick to support his contention. But no oath could erase the testimony of her own eyes. She had seen the medallion and held it in her hands. His guilt this time was irrefutable.

The growing trust her love for him had evoked crashed to her feet like slivers of broken china. Her head throbbed, and her throat felt parched. No amount of velvet charm could compensate for such a lack of personal integrity. It was impossible to condone such behavior under any circumstances. How could she have ever fallen in love with such a man? Any kind of future together was out of the question.

Marnie had no idea how long she sat huddled in the lounge chair, her thoughts spinning a web of disillusion. She only dimly realized that the sun had faded behind the mountains and the children had departed for dinner. Pulling herself to her feet as if she were sleepwalk-